BOUND TO BREAK

MEN OF HONOR

NEW YORK TIMES BESTSELLING AUTHOR

STEPHANIE TYLER

WRITING AS

SE JAKES

This is a work of fiction. Names, characters, places and incidents are the product of the author's imagination or are used fictitiously. Any resemblance to actual persons, living or dead, business establishments, events or locales is entirely coincidental or has been used in a fictional manner.

MEN OF HONOR, BOOK 6

Four men fighting against their pasts…and for each other.

Several years after washing up on a beach in South Africa with absolutely no memory—not even his name—Lucky would rather *not* remember his past. Based on the number of scars on his body, it couldn't have been anything good.

Then a man claiming to be his former Navy SEAL teammate walks into the bar and insists that Lucky's real name is Josiah Joshua Kent. Turns out he's been listed as KIA, and since he's not dead, he's now considered a deserter.

Discovering Josh is alive throws Rex, and his relationship with Sawyer, into a tailspin. Rex can finally lay to rest the nightmares of the night he couldn't save his teammate. And Sawyer is faced with his *worst* nightmare—a relationship threatened by a very real ghost from the past.

As Josh begins to piece his memories back together, another man with a shadowy connection to his past—and maybe his heart—holds the key that could free him. Or send him to a traitor's fate.

Warning: Contains rough language, rougher sex and warriors who fall hard for one another.

This one's for my fabulous editor, Jennifer Miller, who loved the story as much as I did.

PROLOGUE

It was too dark to see, the air so humid it threatened to drown him in the enclosed space. His head throbbed, his body had gone numb weeks ago. And there was no end in sight.

He couldn't stand—the cell was maybe four feet tall and eight feet wide, at best, and the claustrophobia closed in on him minute by minute, so much so that he'd started to look forward to the beatings because at least he was freed then. And upright, strapped to a T-bar while he was whipped, questions screamed at him in between that he never goddamned answered.

You don't know how much you can handle until you're forced to handle it.

That statement had too much truth to it. Especially when his captors dangled the eternal carrot in front of him and his teammates, day in and day out.

"If you help us, your friends can go."

Night after night, he pondered the truth in that statement when he knew there really was none. But lack of food and sleep did strange things to a man, and no amount of training could've ever thoroughly prepared him for this.

For this kind of torture, you were either able to make it through or you weren't. Simple as that. It was a mental game…unless your body broke down physically. After that, all bets were off.

None of them wanted to scream but sometimes the screams slipped out. He'd listen for other signs of suffering— the fast breathing, the grunts that came out involuntarily after being hit too hard.

The terrorists with ties to the FARC were looking for the same intel they'd killed a CIA agent for—wanted a terrorist released from prison in exchange for the second agent's life. He knew that because his team had been sent in to rescue that agent.

There was no sign of the agent, not before or after the SEAL team had been captured.

"You'll cooperate."

He looked up, stared into the face of his captor. "You will cooperate."

"No," he managed.

"One of your friends is already dead because you wouldn't cooperate."

He couldn't answer that. Wouldn't. He was dragged out, but far less roughly. His head spun. His body was too weak, and the men half carried him into a small room he'd never been let into before. And they hadn't taken him past his teammates' cells this time.

He had no idea if they were getting out of this alive. He did know that if they did, they'd never be the same.

There were a lot of people looking to get laid in the packed bar that night, and Lucky wanted to be one of them. The lights were low, music screamed in his ears and his body moved unconsciously to the beat as he poured drinks and flirted easily with the regulars.

Emme waved him down. "Luck, give me four lemon-drop shots." Emme always called him Luck, short for Lucky, because she'd been the one to name him that after finding him washed up on the beach in the middle of the night.

"I tripped over you and I screamed," Emme told him all the time. "First, I thought it was a dead whale. And then I thought you were just dead."

I was, he always thought when she told that part.

Dead and reborn Lucky on that wet sand on the Easter Cape beach almost four years earlier. He didn't even know how old he was. Didn't know his real name, if his parents were dead or alive.

But the scars that striped across his back and the backs of his thighs told him he'd been through a terrible ordeal. He'd incorporated that into his made-up past, told the doctors and Emme's family—the Bains—that his name was Doug, that he'd been abused as a teen and that he'd emancipated himself and was traveling, doing odd jobs and determined to live life on his terms.

The last part was true enough. He'd told the Bains that he'd gone out too far and the riptide had yanked him.

The thing was, the riptide *had* been there, but he'd instinctively known to swim along with it, parallel to the shore instead of trying to fight it. This was where his memory started—a terrifying moment of waking up submerged in the dark water. He'd been lucky he hadn't inhaled, which spoke of luck.

Or maybe experience.

He'd discovered he knew how to swim seconds after being dumped into the Indian Ocean that night. And he had swum—it had been more sophisticated than panicked survival instinct. Because he hadn't panicked. He'd been exhausted but he'd finally found a place where the current broke and had swum until he hit sand. He'd lain on the beach, freezing, until the Bains had found him. His first instinct on meeting Emme and her parents had been to lie. That had worked out well for him, and he'd remained in South Africa ever since.

He was most likely American, but had no passport, no social security number to prove that, so leaving wasn't on his highest list of priorities. And this pace of life had suited him, at least at first.

Lately, he'd been restless. He guessed having no choices would do that to a man eventually.

"Here you go." He slid the shots down the bar, one by one toward the waiting women. They laughed as they caught the glasses and thanked him. One, a tall, pretty brunette, held up her shot and toasted him before moving to be closer to where he was working. She flirted with him for a few minutes—he returned the banter but he was too busy for anything more.

That was all right—she wasn't his type anyway. "Hey, can I grab a Jack and Coke?"

Lucky looked up into the face of the man who'd placed the order and nodded. "Coming right up."

The guy did a double take. He was good-looking, but Lucky had immediately pegged him for straight. He waited a beat, but the guy suddenly reached across the bar for him, saying, "Josh? Holy fuck—is that really you?"

Lucky put his hands up and backed away.

The name Josh didn't set off any alarm bells, but Lucky would be lying if he hadn't thought about a moment like this constantly. Some days he looked over his shoulder more than others.

Tonight, his defenses had been down. His gut told him to move this away from the bar, take it outside so Emme wouldn't see it happening. He pushed out, calling, "Taking ten," and didn't wait to hear her agree.

The big blond guy followed him. When Lucky turned to face him under the lights in the adjacent alleyway, he noted the guy looked like he'd seen a ghost. "How the hell did you escape?"

"I'm not Josh," he said.

"You're Josh Kent. Come on, I'd know you anywhere," the guy started again, softer this time, like one might talk to a wounded animal. He kept his hands to himself, tucked them into his jeans pockets to make himself appear less threatening.

But Lucky was threatened. Half of him fought a tremble but the other half was ready to throw down. Instinct made him react, forced him to keep a wide berth between the two of them. "You've got the wrong guy."

But he persisted. "Josh, it's Nate. We served together."

Fuck. Served together. He'd long suspected he'd been in the military, but he played dumb instead, hoping it was all a case of mistaken identity. "Served drinks?"

"In the Navy."

"My name's Lucky, not Josh. Sorry." He went to turn away but Nate grabbed his upper arm forcefully and spun him around.

"Four years, Josh. We all thought you died. We watched you…fuck…we watched you die and now you're hanging out bartending?" Nate let go of him, put his hands up as if apologizing. "If you don't remember…"

"I don't know what you're talking about." Lucky pushed

at him, his palms against the big guy's shoulders, and Nate stumbled back.

"Strong as ever, you dumb fuck. Why the hell are you hiding here?"

"You need to leave," Lucky said, but Nate was charging for him, angry now. He braced but Nate stopped when another man stepped in between them.

That guy was also big and broad, and for a horrible second, Lucky thought he was on Nate's side. But he put himself in front of Lucky and told Nate, "You need to back off."

"You don't understand—I know him," Nate said.

"He doesn't know you. He's said so. Chalk it up to a case of mistaken identity."

"It's not," Nate insisted. "I'll leave now—but I'll be back with proof. You're Josh Kent." He pointed at Lucky and then stormed off.

Lucky walked over to the nearest car and sat on the hood. Sweat trickled down his back and he took a deep breath. He'd built a web of lies about who he was. All this time, he hadn't told anyone he couldn't remember shit about his past. And really, how would they know?

He didn't tell them because they'd make him deal with it, and he was pretty damned sure he didn't want to go there again. Ever.

"He scared the hell out of you," his savior said, his voice rough. So was his hand that reached out to touch him, but the good rough that made Lucky feel something. The calming hand rested on the back of his neck, centered him, allowed him to simply bow his head and take a deep breath.

The hand remained there for what seemed like hours but was really just minutes. He finally raised his head and the guy's hand slid off.

Lucky missed the contact. "I'm okay. I've been fighting a flu," he lied, because that's apparently what he did best. "Thanks for that—I just wasn't up to dealing with a stalker."

"Is that what he was?"

He looked into the pale blue eyes that seemed to want truth and barely managed, "Yeah."

"Well, any employee of my family's bar is typically like family." He blinked. "You're Dashiell."

"Dash."

In all these years, he'd never met Emme's brother, an award-winning photographer. Emme said he always avoided being photographed himself, just let his work speak for him. There were a lot of his prints around Lucky's apartment, haunting pictures of people and places in third-world countries. Lucky was always drawn to them as though he'd been there, looking over his shoulder as the pictures were taken. Like he had a connection to Dash, which was ridiculous.

"I've seen your photographs. Great stuff." He sounded like an idiot. Blamed Nate for riling him up and tried to calm down. "Emme always brags about you."

"She's good for that," Dash agreed. He wore his blond hair long, tied back. The stubble on his face looked like it would be rough too if Lucky rubbed his hand against it. There was a scar on his chin that Lucky wanted to trace down to his neck. Looked dressed down, like he'd blend in anywhere. But he was just handsome enough to be memorable.

Lucky didn't know why he did that—catalogued people quickly, studied, looking and assessing for strengths and weaknesses—but he did it all the damned time.

You were in the Navy.

"Speaking of Emme, I need to get back in there." Lucky slid off the car, and Dash put a hand on his shoulder, as if to steady him. Whether he'd needed it or not, he liked the way it felt.

Dash walked into his family's bar a step behind Lucky, tamping down the adrenaline that threatened to take over his body. For a second before he entered, he closed his eyes and mentally compared the old picture from the file to the man he'd had his hands on.

It was hard not to reach out and touch the guy again, and he cursed himself for even doing so in the first place. It wasn't the reaction he'd pictured having when he'd finally been proven correct in believing that Josh Kent—aka "Lucky"—was alive.

Alive, with a possible terrorist connection and living with your family.

Lucky didn't even turn around after he jumped behind the bar and began taking drink orders. Emme went to say something to him but spotted Dash and ran over to him instead. He noted that Lucky looked relieved. "Finally! I was beginning to think you'd disowned us."

He hugged her back. "Sorry—work's been keeping me busy."

"I know. I collect your work, remember?" She swatted him with the towel she'd had tucked in her jeans and they walked to the back room where it was quieter. "Please tell me you're sticking around for a little while."

"At least a couple of days."

"I see you met our best bartender." She motioned over her shoulder at Lucky.

He took a deep breath and held back, because scaring the shit out of his sister—or letting Lucky know he was suspicious—was the last thing Dash wanted to do. "Yep. Lucky's an unusual first name."

"It's a nickname—we gave it to him when we rescued him."

Dash crossed his arms and waited for the story. "Okay, not so much rescued him, because he was fine, but he'd been swimming and he'd fallen asleep on the beach and he was freezing."

"And so you and Mom and Dad decided to add him to

the family tree?"

"We took him to hospital when we couldn't wake him up. He didn't have any ID on him and he looked like…" She shook her head, stopped her train of thought. "Anyway, he's a good guy. Helps with stuff around the bar and the house too. Never missed work. He's honest and the customers love him."

Dash could see that. Lucky was a tall, good-looking guy. His dark hair was done in a messy fashion—not too long, not too short. Good hair. Serious dark-brown eyes.

Dash had seen Lucky struggling with his anger when Nate questioned him, had watched him flex his hands as though unconsciously preparing for hand-to-hand combat.

He'd had the right stance for it. Even if he hadn't known who Lucky really was, Dash would've said he was no goddamned bartender…not until he'd backed off and acted like he was on the verge of a panic attack.

It was like he'd been fighting a part of himself. "He's using the apartment," Emme continued. "My apartment?"

"You haven't been home in six years."

"But I'm here now." He blew out a frustrated breath.

There was definitely something going on with Lucky, but the guy had been here for four years and he'd done nothing. He was staying in Dash's apartment—he knew who Dash was. Four years and he hadn't made his move. It didn't make sense.

Dash's family had to pay Lucky in cash, unless he'd had

the means to get a fake ID and start a bank account. But if he had an ID, why stay in one place for four years? Why not hide?

Unless he'd decided on hiding in plain sight.

Dash had been in these circles too long not to notice when something wasn't right. Obviously, his family hadn't inherited any of his situational awareness, but they were used to *him* being suspicious. Emme always attributed it to him working in some of the world's most dangerous places, and she was right. But she only knew half his truth. His photography was a convenient cover story for his other work, the kind you could never tell family about without putting them at risk.

He'd stayed away so he wouldn't do that. And now, he discovered that his family had invited a risk to live and work with them. A man Dash had been searching for.

You've got the wrong guy.

He'd never thought this moment would actually come, not like this, with a man who appeared to have no memory of who he was. Dash had been the only one to believe Josh Kent might be alive. Sometimes, being right wasn't all it was cracked up to be.

"You can stay at the house," Emme told him.

No way. "I'll talk to Lucky. Maybe he'll let me crash in the extra room for a few nights."

Emme's face was unreadable, but all she said was, "It's closing time—I've got to do last call. Then we'll talk more."

Yes, they would.

He watched Lucky and Emme interact. Lucky was still shaken—he couldn't hide that—but there was an easy chemistry between him and Emme that was plain as day. Lucky was protective of her, and in turn, she made him smile. There was a rhythm between the two of them behind the bar that spoke of long nights working together, a closeness that Dash himself didn't have with his sister any longer.

Unable to shake off the melancholy that mixed in with the unease, he tore his eyes away from Lucky and looked around the old place. He guessed it was true that the more things changed, the more they stayed the same. The bar was in a perfect spot to attract all the locals but just upscale enough to keep the tourists pouring in. Most were dressed casually, some still in cover-ups over their bathing suits.

Last call was more raucous than usual. Dash was glad. It allowed him to slip out again and wait in the parking lot for Nate.

Nate, whom he'd been tracking for the past four years, because he traveled the most out of the three SEALs who'd returned home after the capture. He wasn't disappointed. He'd been outside maybe five minutes when the guy was back, storming across the dusty parking area. When he saw Dash, he stopped short, then motioned for Dash to come with him around the side of the bar.

This was the first time Dash had actually gotten on a

plane and followed him. That was because he'd made plans to come to Dash's hometown, his family.

Yes, Nate surfed all over the world, and this beach was a well-known surfing spot. But for Dash, he couldn't risk it simply being a coincidence—not with his family involved.

"How well do you know Lucky?" Nate asked without preamble. "I don't."

"I do." Nate handed him his phone and Dash paged through several photos. Lucky, standing next to Nate, in jungle BDUs. Lucky, hugging a guy with a shaved head, looking happy. "That's Rex. He and Josh lived together."

"Did you tell him anything?"

Nate's expression tightened. "It would kill him if I'm wrong. It'll kill him anyway."

"Unless Josh Kent has a twin…" Dash trailed off.

"I worked with him for years. I know who that is—I'd know him anywhere." Nate paused. "We thought we lost him on a mission four years ago."

"Torture?"

Nate nodded. "I saw him die."

"Scars?"

Nate lifted his chin. "We were captured. Tortured. He was killed. Burned."

"Guessing it wasn't him."

"Obviously. We never looked for a body because we all saw it burn."

"So he might've been tortured for as long as you guys.

Maybe longer. Escaped. Lost his memory along the way."

"Check him for scars—lots of them. Like this." Nate turned, lifted his shirt and showed broad stripes that would never heal. "They'd be on the backs of his thighs too. And he's burned. His lower back, below the waistline. Plus a scar on his calf." He lowered his shirt and turned back.

"You're retired?"

"Yes."

Nate had retired willingly. Whether he passed psych evals or not wasn't disclosed. Uncle was another SEAL on that team who'd been forced into retirement after a long medical leave because his arms hadn't healed right from the torture he'd been put through. Rex was still active duty with an impeccable record.

"How'd you end up here?"

"I end up in a lot of places," was all Nate said. "What do you do for a living?"

"I'm just a photographer."

"Right." Nate drew out the word. "Look, I know you're going to check me and my story out. Not sure why the hell you're here, if it's dumb luck or if you know about Josh. Either way, our kind recognizes our kind. Don't fuck with me."

Dash shrugged, and for Nate, he guessed that was enough of an answer. The guy might've thought he was a merc too, or retired military or something along those lines, and he'd be damned close to the truth. "Let me feel him out. If he's a lost POW, he needs to deal with it."

Nate nodded. "I've got to report this to the Navy. This is a big goddamned deal. He has classified intel."

Not if he doesn't have a memory. "Give me twenty-four hours."

"What are you going to do?"

"See if I can figure out if he's for real or if he's a deserter. He's been living and working with my family."

"The Josh I knew was a good guy."

"People change," Dash said.

Dash wasn't anywhere in sight when Lucky left the bar and headed to the apartment he rented from Emme's family. It was above the bar, and the bar was about twenty feet from the main house. It was all circled by private gates and twenty-four-hour security.

It was Emme's night to close and Lucky didn't hang around to help, like he did sometimes. Instead, he locked himself in the apartment, the music she kept on loud still making the floor under him shake.

He poured himself a tall drink and downed half of it in a single gulp. His hands trembled when he thought about what Nate had told him in the parking lot.

Four years, Josh. We all thought you died... If you don't remember...

Four years ago next week, he'd washed up on the beach. Four years, and the scars had barely faded.

"I don't remember," he said out loud, the frustration in his voice surprising him.

The knock on the door didn't startle him, but it came

sooner than he'd thought. When he opened it, he wasn't surprised to see Dash there, but he was grateful it wasn't Nate.

"This is your place," he said as a greeting, and Dash nodded and asked, "Mind if I stay in the second bedroom?"

"That's where I stay. Didn't touch your room." He moved aside to let Dash in and locked the door tight behind them.

"You could've." Dash had a single bag with him and he dropped it on the floor next to the couch.

"Wasn't right." He'd left the place exactly as he'd found it, all Dash's pictures on the walls. Closed the door to his room. Emme's mom sent someone in to clean weekly and Lucky supposed she dusted and such in there, but he never checked. He already felt like he'd invaded the guy's privacy by looking through the books of photographs Dash had left, but he couldn't stop himself. He felt like they were helping him, even if he didn't understand why.

"You okay?" Dash asked.

"Not really." He finished the rest of the drink and poured more whiskey into the glass. "Want some?"

"Shouldn't drink if you're coming down with the flu."

"Drowns all the bad shit out of you," Lucky offered.

"Not all of it." Dash's expression had gone hard. Lucky touched his face before he could stop himself, then slid a hand around to his neck.

"Then what does?"

"If I'd figured that out…" Dash paused, and then brought

his mouth down on Lucky's. Lucky responded immediately, his hands on Dash's shoulders as Dash put his arm around Lucky's waist, pulling him close.

Lucky's entire body jackknifed under the contact, Dash's arms the only thing holding him up. He could blame the drink or the stress, but really, the rough touch and the handling always did it for him.

Dash pulled back and studied him for a long moment, then rubbed the rough of his cheek against Lucky's. Lucky shivered and Dash chuckled.

"I like it rough. Can't seem to find that around here," Lucky confessed. "Tonight's your lucky night."

Lucky laughed. "Lucky's lucky."

"And drunk."

"Not so bad," he managed before Dash was kissing him again, hard and fast. Ripping off Lucky's T-shirt and letting it fall to the floor. The man's touch was fire on his skin, fingertips digging in, ignoring the scars he had to have felt. He just wanted the pleasure, no background or complications.

"Good?" Dash asked.

"Can't tell?" he panted back, ground his jean-covered cock against Dash's leg. "Am I screwed because I'm fucking the boss's son?"

"Screwed being the operative word," Dash murmured while unzipping Lucky's jeans. He gasped when Dash covered his cock with his hand. "I don't fuck and tell."

He didn't care if or what he did as long as Dash kept stroking his cock. His hips jutted forward, his entire body seeking a contact he hadn't had in forever.

It was familiar, but unlike anything he'd had recently. He couldn't recall his sexual past any more than he could his name, but he knew he liked cock. And he knew he liked it rough.

Finally, someone *got* him. "Not gonna last."

"Who said I want you to?" Dash told him, but he stopped stroking and instead ran a finger across the head of his cock, smearing precome over it.

"Don't tease—not now."

Dash's smile was slow and lazy. "Take your jeans off."

Lucky did, carefully, because he didn't want to lose any of Dash's contact on his cock, no matter how light. When he'd finally managed to kick them off, he tried to hold himself steady against the wall, but that was getting harder to do.

It got even more so when Dash let go of him only to put his hands on Lucky's shoulders and spin him around. His palms hit the wall, Dash kicked his legs apart and ran a hand over his ass. "Perfect. Stay that way until I find some lube."

"Top dresser drawer."

He closed his eyes, pressed his cheek against the wall and then remembered that his scars were in full goddamned view. He went to turn but Dash's hand was back on his shoulder, pressing him into place.

"Relax. I already saw them. They don't make me want to fuck you any less." Dash's lubed finger ran along his crack slowly, traced his hole before pressing inside, fast, to the knuckle.

He opened his mouth to tell Dash that he'd lost the mood, that he didn't goddamned want to do this anymore, but then two fingers opened him, stroked his gland, and he didn't want anything other than Dash to fuck him. Hard. Now.

He shuddered as Dash added a third finger, turned his face forward and screwed his eyes shut so he could get totally lost in this. Forget that anything else happened tonight except this.

"You need another drink?" Dash asked him.

He was intoxicated from the whiskey, its effects furthered by Dash's efforts. He lost himself in the rhythm of Dash's hand, his body shuddering. "Come on, fuck me."

But Dash kept up his maddening pace, which wasn't anywhere near fast enough for Lucky. He pushed back against the man's hand and Dash chuckled against his ear. "So fucking impatient. Are you always like this?"

"Haven't had anyone this good touch me in a long time."

"How long?"

"At least a year. So hurry up and keep changing that."

Dash turned him back around, fast, but Lucky was ready. Wrapped a leg around Dash's hip and let the man's cock breach him.

Dash was taller, so it worked perfectly. Lucky lowered himself a little onto Dash's cock so he could be filled faster, and then straightened. Stilled for a brief second after the initial pain of the intrusion and then began to rock toward Dash. "Yeah, just like that," he told the man, and Dash smiled and watched his face as he lost himself in the pleasure haze of sex.

He didn't even realize he was climbing Dash until he found himself hanging on for dear life to the guy, both legs wrapped around Dash. Helpless to do anything but take Dash's thrusts, and fuck, he didn't want this to end.

Like Dash had read his mind, he slowed down, still giving Lucky the zings of pleasure he'd craved. His fingers dug in, he was sure he was leaving nail marks in Dash's skin.

He was also sure Dash didn't mind at all. Because the man kissed him then, and Lucky let himself be devoured, losing himself in the rough touches and the demanding kiss. And after being suspended like that, between orgasm denial and the pleasure Lucky gained from it, Dash seemed to be the one who lost control first. Lucky watched as he pulled back and slammed his hips back and forth hard, how his neck muscles corded with tension as he forced Lucky's orgasm, his following behind by mere seconds.

Lucky let out a long, stuttered moan, mixed with Dash's name—was pretty sure he was yelling his ass off but he didn't care—as his entire body lost control. His cock spurted between their bodies, Dash leaned in and bit him on the chest and that only served to make Lucky's climax last longer. Or maybe he had more than one—he'd lost track.

When he opened his eyes, he found Dash staring at him.

"You okay?" he asked, showing no signs of either pulling out of Lucky or letting the man down.

"We have to do that again."

Dash simply smiled, picked Lucky up easily and got them both to the couch. It was oversized, but there was some maneuvering Dash did to get them both to fit. And they did fit, because they were still connected, and Dash was still on top of him.

Lucky kept his ankles locked around Dash's lower back, urging him deeper. There was no way Lucky would come again this soon, although he felt like he could. Dash took his hips and pulled Lucky into him. Hard. Fast. The slapping sounds filled the room, Lucky's groans keeping pace, and Dash grimaced as he came, like the orgasm actually hurt him.

He dropped Lucky's hips, put his hands down on either side of Lucky's head and lowered his body slowly. Lucky ran his hands over the smooth skin of Dash's back. A shudder went through the man at the touch, and then a soft chuckle of laughter before he raised his head.

"Hope you can breathe, because I can't move," he admitted.

"Been a while for you too, huh?" Lucky asked.

"Holed up in Cambodia for three months. A lot of action, but not the right kind," Dash told him, then put his head down again.

The intoxication of the sex overtook Lucky with far greater pleasure than the drinking had. He didn't need to breathe. He simply wanted Dash to stay like that for as long as he wanted to. And then, longer than that.

The scars Dash knew he'd find were there, all over Lucky's back and the backs of his thighs. Lucky hadn't seemed self-conscious about them at first. Maybe because he was drunk, but more likely because he didn't remember how they'd been put there.

But then he'd remembered them and Dash had to distract him, gently.

He didn't know why he was suddenly oddly protective of Lucky, but it gave credence to Lucky's lack of memory. Dash wasn't a man who was easily fooled. And while he hadn't found any evidence that Nate, Uncle or Rex were involved in terrorist activities, he hadn't been able to let it rest. Not while his gut had never let him believe that Josh Kent was dead.

Good to know he could still trust his instincts.

Now, while they both came down from the sex that had gone on for hours—and Dash wasn't going to pretend he hadn't wanted it—he glanced over at Lucky. The man was lying on his stomach, his cheek turned to the couch pillow, his eyes closed.

He wasn't sleeping, but he was close to it. And his body was a mess of scars, and not just the ones on his back. The guy lived a rough life. Dash put his palm over a healed bullet hole, noted another slash across Lucky's arm that looked like it had come from a knife. "Looks like this hurt."

Lucky lifted his head to see where Dash was touching. Which was…odd, because getting shot wasn't something you forgot readily. He pointed to the hole, and an odd expression crossed Lucky's face before he said dismissively, "I had a rough childhood."

"Rougher than most, looks like."

Lucky looked like he was going to say something else, but he dropped his head to the pillow, burrowing against the pillow with his cheek. Finally, he said, "Can we not talk about that shit?"

"Why's that?"

"Because we just fucking met, man. We've just fucked. I've already had a rough night—can't I just continue to relax? Don't I deserve that?"

Dash brushed a hand over Lucky's cheek and grabbed a bottle of water from the side table to hand to him. "You can relax, but that doesn't mean I'm done fucking you."

"Yeah, I'm cool with that." Lucky took a gulp of water and then drained the bottle. "I'm losing my buzz."

"Can't let that happen." Dash grabbed the whiskey bottle from the coffee table and handed it to Lucky. Lucky took a long swig and handed it to Dash, who did the same.

"How long are you here for?" Lucky asked.

"Sick of me already?"

"Dude, it's your place. Stay as long as you want."

"Emme said you've been here for about four years."

"Emme said you've been gone for six," Lucky countered.

"Job keeps me moving."

"I meant what I said—your pictures are great. I'd like to go to some of those places you photographed."

"Like where?"

Lucky shrugged. "The ones of Malaysia are cool. I'd also like to travel around Africa more, but Emme keeps me working. Plus, it's fun as shit here."

Dash smiled, because Lucky was right about that. It would've been so easy for him to get stuck here, to hang out and tend bar with Emme and spend his nights drinking and fucking and inheriting the family business. Definitely not the worst thing to happen to a guy. "Emme likes having you around."

"She talks about you all the time, you know. She misses the hell out of you."

Dash shoved that guilt down and wondered how he'd allowed Lucky to lecture him when he was supposed to be the interrogator. Instead, he found himself saying, "It's hard to pass up opportunities."

"When you photograph a spot, how long do you spend there?"

"Why? You planning on taking my job?"

"Maybe."

Dash angled himself, threw a leg over Lucky's. "I don't plan anything when I'm on a job. I find things work out better that way. I just show up, start getting a feel for the place. Sometimes, I don't take pictures right away—I just hang out, getting the lay of the land. Checking the people out."

It was exactly what he did, but for the CIA and not for the national magazines that ran his pictures. That second part was a happy accident when his cover story ended up making waves in the magazine world. At first, his supervisor had been pissed, but then he'd decided it was probably the best cover story ever.

It had worked for the past ten years. Dash got to combine something he loved with adventure and danger, which were other things he loved just as much. It was a win-win. What sucked was not being able to explain it to his family.

"So, you want to bartend for the rest of your life?" he asked Lucky, who groaned.

"Seriously? You're going to give me the ambition speech? I'm happy as fuck."

Dash slid off the couch and picked Lucky up. At first, he struggled, but when he realized where Dash was headed, he stopped. Dash kicked open the door to his bedroom—the first time in six years—and dumped Lucky onto his bed.

Lucky propped himself up on his elbows and looked around at the pictures lining the wall.

"You've really never been in here?" Dash asked.

"I don't invade anyone's private space."

"Well, now I've invited you. Feel free to check out the pictures. But not now."

Lucky smirked as Dash yanked him closer, bit his neck again. Leaving another mark on Lucky, like he was sixteen and couldn't help himself. It was like he knew his time with Lucky was limited and he was trying to live a lifetime in one night.

He tried to push the fact that he didn't want this to be for just one night into the back of his mind. Because this was supposed to be a goddamned job. And somehow, it had turned into something else altogether.

All for the job, Dash, he tried to tell himself and even he didn't believe his own bullshit this time.

"Do you think that that guy's going to come back and bother you?" he asked now.

"Not sure," Lucky mumbled. "Hope not."

"Does that happen to you a lot?"

"No," Lucky told him. "Guess I have a twin somewhere."

There was no guile in his eyes, but Dash couldn't shake the fact that Lucky knew something big was coming down the line for him.

If Lucky did have amnesia, he'd have to know he had

zero memories. And he'd have to be waiting for his past to catch up with him, maybe every day of his life.

3

Several hours later, after Lucky had passed out, Dash stared at the clock and wondered what the hell he'd been thinking. Never thought he'd be this close to anyone from this SEAL team. Now that he was, his entire mission seemed to have taken a hard shift to the right, and he was barely holding on.

He slid out of bed, dragged on his jeans and shirt and left the apartment barefoot. Nate was waiting outside the closed bar. The retired SEAL was smoking a cigarette, held the pack out to Dash, who took one, lit it and watched the smoke float around them.

Since he only allowed himself to smoke after sex, he'd practically quit. And, since he couldn't count using his hand for sex. If he did that, he'd have a hell of a habit.

"You checked me out?" Nate asked finally. "Because if you have that kind of clearance, you're CIA."

Dash didn't answer. Couldn't. Didn't have to.

It didn't matter. "I came here for vacation. Can't fucking believe I stumbled on this shit. I've got enough to do," Dash told him instead.

Whether Nate believed that or not wasn't Dash's concern.

"I came here to surf," Nate said. "My other former teammate—Uncle—he's meeting me here in the morning. Was supposed to come to surf too but…"

Dash recalled reading that the two men—Uncle especially—were excellent surfers. Uncle's injuries to his arms had made it difficult but not impossible to continue doing so. And there was a surfing competition happening here in the next week, so it was either a brilliant cover story or the truth. Dash knew from experience that sometimes those things were one and the same. "Guess this throws a wrench into those plans."

"Little bit," Nate agreed. "You think Josh really has amnesia?"

"I can't be sure of anything except for the fact that he's definitely Josh Kent."

"I already told you that." Nate sounded sad and disgruntled at once.

Dash also had Lucky's fingerprints that matched those of Josh Kent—he'd sent those to his supervisor an hour before—but he didn't tell Nate that.

He wanted to shake Lucky, to pin him to the car and ask him why the hell he'd come here, near Dash's family. Wanted to torture the shit out of him to get him to admit what Dash wanted to hear.

Except he didn't know what the hell it was that he wanted

Lucky to say anymore, because somehow, in the space of mere hours, he'd started feeling like Lucky was innocent. And at this point, Dash's gut feelings wouldn't be taken into account by the Navy, so instead of blowing his mission, he simply told Nate, "Josh's freaked out. He didn't come out and say it, but if he can't remember anything…"

"Yeah, I mean, if he knows enough to realize that he's missing memories, missing everything, that's got to be scary as hell," Nate said.

Dash flashed to Lucky's face and how panicked he'd gotten when Nate had confronted him. By all accounts, including Emme's, he wasn't violent but rather a consistently calm guy. "Time'll tell. If he's playing us, he'll reveal himself sooner or later. No one's that good."

"Not even you?" Nate asked.

Dash pressed his lips together, then told him, "Might want to let the Navy know you're bringing him in. Up to them if they charge him with UA or Desertion."

"Fuck." Nate took another drag of his cigarette. "I'll report it now. Unless you already did."

"You gave me the time. Figured I'd let you do the honors."

Nate stared at him. "Why're you doing this?"

Dash thought about lying. About giving some blithe answer and walking away. But his body reacted fiercely and he lunged at Nate, grabbed his collar. Told him, "Because you're all too close to my family for goddamned comfort. And if you've got any plans, I've got your teammate."

Nate stared at him, his expression pained. "You're definitely CIA."

Nate's words didn't require an answer, and Dash wouldn't have given one anyway.

Nate shook his head slowly, said, "It's you. You're the agent who escaped before we infiltrated and got captured ourselves."

Dash let go of him and continued to keep his mouth shut. He'd said what he needed to.

But Nate hadn't. "Touch Josh and I'll kill *you*. Because his capture came when he was rescuing your ass. And that's all you need to know. Other than that, I get it. I get it all too well." Nate turned and walked away without looking back, and yes, of course he'd understand. Lucky—*Josh*—would be considered a criminal until he could prove he wasn't.

Finding him alive was only the first step, and the rest of the flight could be a steep drop down for all of them.

He went back into the house. Lucky still slept, curled around the pillows, and the spot Dash had vacated was still there. He swallowed hard and parked himself in the chair under the window instead. Flicked through the TV since he was too worked up to sleep… and was proven wrong when he woke with Lucky standing over him, talking to him quietly and calmly.

The screams he'd thought were coming from the TV had been his.

"Fuck. Fuck," he ground out and pushed a trembling

hand through his hair. The nightmare came rushing back to him in seconds, the road, the jungles, seconds before he and Jim had been grabbed.

He'd woken up just after they'd shot Jim. And he hadn't had this—or any nightmare—in years. He always slept without issue, could only blame the proximity of the man who may or may not be threatening his family.

If he closed his eyes, he could see the writing inside the file.

Josh Kent is an excellent liar.

He also had no firearms or weapons, at least none Dash could find. And even though Lucky himself was a deadly weapon, and he seemed to know it on some level, he also seemed not to like it.

So if Josh Kent was still an excellent liar, Dash would be better. He'd slept with men and women for the job, never had qualms, never worried about them. And he certainly never got attached.

With Lucky, he was four for four, and he couldn't do anything about it except let Lucky feed him sips of water, wipe him down while he was sweating and putting blankets on him when his skin got clammy.

"If you didn't want me to stay in here with you, could've just told me," Lucky said. "You shouldn't have to sleep in a chair in your own room."

"Wasn't that. Wasn't you," Dash said and realized he wasn't lying.

Lucky was staring at him in the partial darkness, his head tilted like he was trying to get a read on Dash. "I'm trying not to take it personally, but it's not easy."

"You don't have nightmares?"

"I don't dream," Lucky admitted. He pursed his lips together for a second, like he was worried about what he'd said.

"Never?"

"No, never. What's it like?" he asked.

"Well, obviously, that one I just had wasn't good."

"Yeah, right. Sorry. Look, I'll just go back into my room and…"

My room. Not the other room, but *my room.* Like he belonged there. Because he so obviously did.

"You can stay here," he said. Lucky hesitated and Dash stood, pointed to the bed. "I want you to stay here."

Lucky nodded, climbed back under the covers and Dash followed. Knew he'd never go back to sleep tonight, no matter how tired he was.

Lucky put his arms around Dash and pulled him to his chest. Rubbed a hand through his hair.

"Dreams are like…they're tough for anyone who doesn't like to lose control. Because even if it's a good dream, you want to live it, and you can't. You're you in the dream, but it's like watching yourself as you hover above."

"Like Ebenezer Scrooge, when the ghosts of Christmas let him look at different times in his life, and he's yelling at himself but no one can hear him?" Lucky asked.

"Yeah, exactly like that."

Scrooge had always been Emme's favorite Christmas movie. The family had to endure it a million times during every holiday season, and there was a fondness in Lucky's voice as he'd talked about it.

How good did you have to be to fake that kind of shit?

Because telling Dash he didn't dream wasn't exactly a slip—not really. It happened sometimes with head injuries, for sure. But telling Dash was a slip—it let him know Lucky realized he was missing things, that Lucky was just waiting for this moment to happen, for his past to catch up with him.

In a few hours, it would be time to deal with all sorts of consequences. For now, Dash buried his head against Lucky's chest and pushed a hand between the man's legs. Maybe sex didn't always make everything better and maybe it did, but it had been too good before not to chance it.

"Your pictures became my dreams," Lucky told him in the dark. "Jesus, I sound stupid. Blame it on the drinks."

"That's a hell of a compliment, Lucky."

"How is it possible to feel close to someone you've never met?"

"And now that you've met me?" Dash asked, didn't expect the answer he got from a soft-spoken Lucky.

"As good as I thought it'd be."

Even as the warning bells rang in Dash's head, he ignored

them. Pushed them aside because he didn't want to admit what the hell he was feeling.

Maybe it's only because you know what he's been through.

"You're going to leave soon." It wasn't a question.

"My job doesn't let me stay in one place for long," Dash said.

"I love it here."

That was obvious. So much so, it made Dash ache. "It's hard to leave."

"So you don't visit often because of that?"

"I think that's probably it."

"Your parents come back the day after tomorrow," Lucky told him. "I'm betting Emme's already sounded the horn that you're here."

Dash smiled. He was sure of that too. The fact that Dad was traveling meant he was in better health than he'd been last year. "Were you around when Dad had the heart attack?"

Lucky's face darkened. "I heard your mom yelling. I was in the storeroom. He was on the floor of the bar. He wasn'tbreathing."

Dash stared at him. "You saved him."

"I did what anyone would've done."

That wasn't true, but Dash's throat was too tight to get the words out. He lay there in silence until he could tell Lucky, "I didn't even know Dad had a heart attack until he was through surgery. They called but I was unreachable."

"They know the opportunities you get are once in a lifetime. They're so proud of you. Sometimes, I think they might be more excited than you about your jobs."

"You took care of my family. I was supposed to be there."

"You couldn't be. So I was."

"I can't ever thank you enough for that."

Lucky stared up at the light patterns on the ceiling. "I've been thinking about how there's a reason for everything. How we ultimately end up exactly where we need to be."

"How'd you end up here?"

"You want to see if my story's different from Emme's?"

Dash laughed. "Touché."

Lucky stroked a hand down Dash's bare arm. "No tattoos. Pretty rare."

No one had fucking touched him like this in forever. Goddammit, it felt good. He'd forgotten how much he'd needed a touch—a kind response from someone who gave a shit. "You don't have any either."

Lucky frowned. "Yeah. Just didn't seem like my thing."

Dash swallowed hard, because he knew why there wouldn't be. Most operators didn't like to have any distinguishing marks, anything that would make them recognizable. They needed to be masters of disguise, able to blend in anywhere and everywhere.

Knowing more about Lucky than Lucky himself did about his life made Dash melancholy. Made him rethink his whole plan, especially when Lucky rubbed his shoulders.

Dash stretched gratefully onto his belly, not expecting Lucky to answer his questions. When Lucky said, "I don't remember anything before washing up on the beach and Emme finding me," Dash fought not to turn around and study his face.

Instead, he asked, "Did you talk to the police?"

"No. I went to the hospital—Emme insisted I go to be checked out—and I convinced the doctors that I got disoriented on a night swim, that I was new to the area. That I'd been in an accident days before, and when I wouldn't talk about the marks on my back, they stopped asking."

"But you really have no memory." Dash turned. Lucky was still half straddling his hip. "That must suck."

"Yeah."

"Must be scary."

Lucky smiled a little. "Don't know why I'm telling you. Maybe because I want you to know I'm not here to hurt your family. I'm not some crazy drifter. Then again, I might be. Or maybe this is the first steady job I've ever had. I think about that sometimes. I could've been anyone." He didn't mention Nate or the Navy, but that had to be weighing on his mind.

It was never an official mission for Dash to keep an eye on the three SEALs. But to Dash, it couldn't have been more personal. Because they were set free three days after Josh "died". And that had never made any sense to Dash. From the transcripts he'd read, it hadn't made any sense to

Nate, Uncle or Rex either.

But Dash couldn't not believe Lucky. "Sometimes it's easier to tell a stranger."

"Sometimes you didn't feel like a stranger."

Lucky leaned down and put his mouth on Dash's then, as his hand slid in between Dash's ass cheeks and the other in between their bodies to circle Dash's cock.

He'll never forgive you for what you're doing to him.

And Dash would never forgive himself if he didn't do his job.

4

Four months away on a mission with Rex at the helm of the team, and Sawyer hadn't been able to do more than catch a quick touch with his CO and lover. Things were strictly professional on that front, as professional as anything that was life or death could be.

But now, that professionalism was driving Sawyer crazy. Had been, ever since the plane landed at 0400 and he'd had to wait through the past ten hours to get his physical and finish debriefing.

Finally, he'd gone home and dumped his stuff. Headed for Rex's, and got there before him. He'd pulled his car into the garage, which he'd taken to doing so no one would notice he was at Rex's more often than not.

When the man walked in two hours later, Sawyer didn't hesitate. Jumped him, and Rex grabbed his thighs as he maneuvered Sawyer against the wall, kissing him while he dumped his bag and his keys, the two of them half laughing at how needy they both were.It was a good needy, though. After all this time of being focused solely on their work—

and the mission had been fucking spectacular on their end—to be able to spend this time getting to know each other again was all Sawyer wanted.

"Missed you," he murmured against Rex's mouth. He realized that sounded ridiculous, as he'd woken up next to the man for the past hundred and twenty-one days. But even though they got to know each other on a totally different level every time they went on a mission together, they also lost the romantic piece of their relationship.

It was no different than a long-distance relationship. But reestablishing their intimacy definitely had its perks.

Rex kept kissing him even as he stripped his shirt and tags, did the same for Sawyer before half carrying, half dragging him over to the couch. He must've decided he didn't have the room he needed there, because Sawyer found himself on his hands and knees on the rug, his cargos pulled down roughly, and oh yes, Rex's tongue inside him, taking him, holding him open and helpless.

He rocked back and forth, his dick rubbing nothing but air. He went to grab it but Rex pulled his face away long enough to tell him no before going back to his torture.

"Fuck, Rex, come on…I need to…"

Rex pulled his face away again and before Sawyer could finish his statement, Rex was pressing his cock inside Sawyer. He must've lubed up while he was licking Sawyer, because the slide in, while tight, was eased by the slickness. And Rex wasn't being gentle, probably couldn't be, any more than Sawyer couldn't help but slam back into him.

His eyes watered and he cursed. Drew a deep breath. Rex's hand went to the back of his neck and then rubbed the center of Sawyer's back, between his shoulder blades, forcing him to relax.

Soon, Sawyer's body had adjusted enough for Rex to begin fucking him in earnest. He grabbed Sawyer's cock—finally—and began to stroke it in tandem with his thrusts.

He'd been about to yell Rex's name loud enough to wake the goddamned neighbors—as usual—when the now-familiar ringtone of Rex's phone began to chime. Rex froze and cursed, then rubbed Sawyer's back gently before he extricated himself to take the call.

He always took the calls from his former teammates in another room, but even though the phone stopped ringing while he was on his way to the kitchen, Rex still kept walked away, muttering, "This better be fucking good." And, no doubt, redialing.

In the meantime, Sawyer sat back on his heels, ass and dick aching, his skin chilled from the loss of contact. It seemed like hours before Rex came back, and when he did, it was fast. So fast, Sawyer didn't see him coming, couldn't ask if everything was okay, because Rex was rocking against him again, but he wasn't hard anymore.

Sawyer rose onto his knees again and leaned against the man's chest. "'S'okay," he murmured. In response, Rex took his cock in hand again and stroked Sawyer until his balls tightened with the threat of the imminent orgasm. And Sawyer needed it so badly, he didn't try to pretend that it would've been okay if Rex had stopped everything.

"I've got you, Sawyer. Come on, show me how fucking much you missed me," Rex told him in that low, gruff, commanding voice Sawyer had grown to love. He came all over Rex's fingers, spurting over his own belly and chest, a short, exhausted laugh shuddering through his body at the same time as the release.

Rex pushed him down to the carpet gently, turning him to his side in the process. Wiping him down with a discarded T-shirt and grabbing a blanket from the couch to cover them. Like he knew Sawyer's eyes wouldn't stay open for another second.

And they wouldn't. He drifted, his body relaxed for the first time since before they'd started planning for the mission…until the screams woke him up.

"Rex, come on…wake up."

Rex thrashed. Knew he was suspended between the dream and reality, followed the thread of Sawyer's voice to pull him out.

He wasn't sure how long it took, but when he came to, Sawyer was already rubbing him down with a cool cloth, handing him water, talking to him in soothing tones.

It had been the worst nightmare he'd had in years.

He pushed Sawyer away and grabbed for the couch. With what seemed like too much of a major effort for such a simple task, he yanked himself from the floor and sat on the edge of the cushion, unable to look at the younger SEAL. Finally, he mumbled, "Sorry."

"What's going on?" Sawyer asked. His voice held a slight demand that raised Rex's hackles, but only for a moment. Because of course Sawyer would know something was wrong, considering Rex hadn't been able to finish fucking him after the phone call he'd received. And Rex had been so goddamned turned around, he hadn't known what the hell to do with himself, so he'd distracted Sawyer until he'd fallen asleep.

And he should've known better than to follow Sawyer into dreamland.

"Rex, man, come on. What's going on?" Sawyer repeated, and Rex thought back to the message from Nate.

"I wasn't going to call you yet, but I have to, man. I think I found Josh. Alive. Holy fuck, Rex—Josh is alive."

Nate's phone had cut off at the end. The country code put Nate in South Africa, and it had taken everything Rex had not to jump on a plane and go find him, especially when Rex hadn't been able to get through to Nate's phone at all last night, not even to text him.

It can't be true.

But Nate knew Josh well. He wasn't the kind of guy to

see ghosts or jump to conclusions. All these years…

He'd spent ten minutes trying to call or text Nate, another five listening to the message on a continuous loop before he'd headed back out to Sawyer.

Sawyer, who was worried as hell.

"I'm okay, Sawyer."

"I don't believe you."

And there was that too. Sawyer knew him intimately, more so these recent months when they'd spent as much time together as they possibly could.

Rex stared down at his phone, which he'd left on the coffee table, with the ringer set to blast. He hadn't heard from Nate again, planned to call him in the morning, to track him down and find out what the fuck was really happening.

He looked into Sawyer's eyes and knew he had to come clean. But instead of telling him, Rex grabbed his phone and played the message from Nate on speakerphone, his eyes never leaving Sawyer's face.

Sawyer paled. Stared at Rex. His mouth opened and closed and he sat on the floor in front of Rex. Rex saw his hands tremble a little before he fisted them.

"Josh. As in…Josh? Your Josh?" Sawyer asked finally.

Your Josh. Jesus. "Yeah, that Josh."

"The capture…I thought…"

"So did we. I don't understand…" He didn't know what else to say except, "It doesn't change anything between us."

That seemed to snap Sawyer back to caretaker mode, erasing all the signs of distress that had marred his expression only moments earlier.

"It changes everything, Rex. Ah, fuck." Sawyer was next to him on the couch then, gathering Rex in his arms, and Rex put his head against his shoulder, grateful to have the comfort. Grateful that Sawyer allowed him to finally be stunned, the way he should be. A thousand questions were running on a constant treadmill through his mind, because this couldn't be happening. Shouldn't be.

"Maybe Nate was drunk and thought it was Josh. Maybe it's a case of wishful thinking," he heard himself mutter, was talking more to himself than Sawyer, trying to convince himself this couldn't be happening.

And not because he didn't want Josh to be safe and sound and alive, for Chrissakes. Because that meant they'd left him behind four years ago.

That chilled Rex to the bone. He started to shake, and Sawyer wound a blanket around him, held him tighter. "No matter what happens, it'll be okay, Rex. But you should go and bring him home. I'm sure he needs you."

Rex lifted his head and stared at his lover of several months. Sawyer was one hundred percent serious. Whatever issues he might have with the entire situation, and Rex was sure there would be many for both of them, none of them were clouding the man's judgment.

"Rex, do you want me to call Clint? I'm sure he's got a

connection to get you there ASAP."

"I think…if this is true, I've got to keep it official."

Official as in, the Navy still owned Josh's ass. And if Josh was UA…or worse…

Rex rubbed his head as it began to ache. "I'm going to have to go in officially and bring Josh back to the brig."

Sawyer let out a breath. Of course he'd have known that the Navy would do that, but knowing it and watching it happen were two different things.

"Why don't you try Nate again?" he suggested.

Rex nodded and Sawyer handed him the phone. It had gotten buried under pillows and the like during his nightmare and now he looked and saw he'd missed some texts, first from Uncle and then one from Nate again.

Confirmed. It's Josh. He might have amnesia. He doesn't remember us, Uncle's read.

Cell towers were down in our area. Didn't want to use another line. The CIA's been tracking us. Me, specifically, Nate had typed. *Navy and CIA will meet us here.*

Rex swallowed hard. "Looks like I'm going to be leaving in the morning. Uncle's already on his way. The Navy and the CIA are expecting us. I can't believe this, Sawyer. It's a miracle. Since it's not a mistake, it's got to be a miracle."

Sawyer smiled, and it was genuine. "I'm glad, Rex. You deserve a miracle."

So simple. Rex wished it could all be this way, and knew that it might never be again.

Tomorrow morning, Rex would start the first leg of his journey to bring his SEAL teammate home. His bags were packed and waiting by the door.

Sawyer wouldn't be able to drive him to base. Too much scrutiny for that. He hadn't even wanted to stay the night at Rex's house, but the man had insisted.

It had been an uneasy evening. Neither man was particularly hungry, but they still each shoveled food into their mouths for lack of anything to really say to each other. As much as Rex tried to reassure him—and Sawyer tried to reassure him that he didn't need reassurance—it wasn't working.

Finally, they'd simply gotten into bed, where Sawyer watched a movie and Rex fell asleep. Sawyer had been surprised at that but figured it was a good thing.

Since Rex had admitted to him that he'd been having nightmares about his time being held prisoner in South America, Sawyer had witnessed many of them firsthand. They were quiet, not what he'd expected at all. When they'd first gotten together, though, Rex would actually wait for Sawyer to fall asleep before he'd get out of bed and go to sleep on the couch. Sawyer would wake alone, stumble into the next room and sleep on top of Rex, just to prove his point. But once Sawyer had started sleeping over more, when they weren't on a mission, Rex wasn't as worried about Sawyer witnessing the nightmares, and they'd been getting better. Rex slept through the night more often than not.

Rex's nightmare earlier that evening had, understandably, been the worst Sawyer had seen. And while Rex typically didn't have more than one nightmare in a single night, this wasn't an ordinary night. Sawyer's mind was still racing with the news, and he'd managed to fall into a light, fitful sleep where he had dreams about Josh Kent. None of them made sense, but in his dreams, Sawyer was running.

Whether it was toward someone or away from something, he didn't know. Maybe he was looking for Rex, but the fog was too thick and he could barely breathe.

He was trying to pull himself out of the dream but couldn't. Not until the growling he heard grew louder. The growl woke him from a not-so-sound sleep, made him sit up with a hard jerk, ready to wrestle a fucking wolf…

Rex's arm slammed up. If Sawyer hadn't moved fast, his nose would've been broken. He braced for Rex to come after him, but the man seemed to be fighting as though he could only be contained in that small space.

Rex clawed at the bedding, fought an invisible enemy. Every time Rex jerked, Sawyer saw the thick scars that ran across Rex's back.

They also striped the back of the man's thighs. "Josh, come on, you gotta wake up."

Sawyer flinched at Rex's words, the raw anxiety wrapped up in them. He should've expected this after the news they'd gotten today.

Now, Sawyer didn't know what the hell to do. "Rex, you're safe. You need to wake up."

Rex stared at him without really seeing him at all. "Josh…"

Sawyer looked nothing like Josh. Polar opposites, actually. But right now, the only person Rex could see was his former lover.

"Yeah, Rex…it's Josh. Come on and wake up." He kept his voice level, not too loud or threatening.

"Josh, we've got to get the hell out of here."

"Rex, yeah, okay…we're good. You're okay."

Rex extended a hand. "Come on."

Sawyer's throat tightened. He grabbed Rex's hand, let the man pull him down to the mattress and hold him. "Thank God you're safe."

Sawyer didn't trust his voice, just nodded as he stared straight ahead over Rex's shoulder. Rex held on to him for dear life and finally drifted back to sleep.

Sawyer didn't get any more shut-eye that night.

5

Rex woke the next morning wrapped around Sawyer, which was good. But that wasn't enough to shake the huge feeling of unease that gnawed in his gut.

And it didn't have everything to do with the fact that he was headed to South Africa to see Josh. Especially because the more awake he got, the more the feeling intensified, as though there was a memory he should have, but didn't.

He looked around the room now and realized something was awry. Everything from the top of his nightstand was on the floor. The sheets were half off the bed, the comforter too…

"Did I miss wild sex last night?" he asked Sawyer, who glanced over his shoulder. A fleeting expression on the man's face made him grow cold. "Yeah."

"What is it?"

Sawyer didn't answer, but he did shift so he was out of Rex's arms and sitting up against the headboard.

"Did I have a nightmare?" Rex persisted.

"Yes."

"A bad one?"

"Pretty bad."

He stroked a hand over Sawyer's hair. "I'm sorry."

"Nothing to apologize for."

"I feel like there's something. Did I hit you?"

"You tried. I've always been faster than you."

"In your dreams," Rex said and Sawyer's start of a smile disappeared. "Come on, you have to tell me."

"You were trying to get out…you called me Josh. Asked me to get into bed with you. Said you were happy I was alive."

Rex swore.

"I get it. I figured something would happen."

"I didn't mean…Sawyer, it's not…"

"Rex you can't control your dreams. Saying you're happy Josh's alive isn't anything to feel bad about."

"You sound so logical, but I know you're hurt."

"Let it go. I'm sure, after you see him… I'm sure after you see him, you'll be fine.

You won't need to dream about him. You'll have him."

Rex was staring at him like he could read his mind. "I'll drop it for now."

"Good. You've got a long couple of days ahead of you. Concentrate on that. Bring Josh home."

"Just because he dreams about the guy doesn't mean he's still in love with him," Jace told Sawyer as he spotted his bench presses at the weight bench later that afternoon in the gym Clint had set up in their house.

Jace was Sawyer's best friend, and he and Clint had been living together for the past six months or so, ever since they'd realized that, despite their jobs, they would find a way to make being together work.

Part of that had been Clint leaving the CIA and going to work for his old CIA partner, who ran a cross between a PI business and a contracting service. Clint got to pick and choose his jobs, which meant he and Jace were able to spend more time together on Jace's off-time.

Lately, their team hadn't had much of that at all. It had been back-to-back missions, which was a big part of the reason Sawyer and Rex had been out of sorts to begin with. Add this in and…

"You would've crushed your fucking neck if I wasn't here," Jace informed him.

Sawyer snapped to and realized how close he'd come to pressing the weight back against his Adam's apple, because he'd completely stopped paying attention. "Shit."

Jace pulled the bar up and set it down safely. He stared down at Sawyer. "You've got to snap the hell out of this."

"Yeah? Like you did?"

"My situation was completely different. And I did have someone come back from the dead," Jace reminded him.

"Yeah, but I have my boyfriend's ex coming back. And they were still together when he disappeared, remember? And Rex had some really bad nightmares."

"Come on, the capture fucked him up, but if Josh comes back..."

"Then what, Jace?"

"Ah, fuck, Sawyer. I don't know what the hell's going to happen. But I do know that Rex loves you."

"I believe that too."

"Then hang on to it."

"I'm trying but fuck, it's still all new. And now..."

And now the guy Rex loves is back.

"You told me he said they weren't perfect," Jace pointed out, because it was obvious what—and who—Sawyer was referring to.

"Who is?"

Jace grunted a reply through his push-ups. "Dude, it's been four years."

"You would've loved Clint still after four years, right?"

That stopped Jace cold. He looked like he wanted to give Sawyer a different answer than, "Right," but Jace wouldn't lie to him. It's why they were as close as they were. That, and the fact that they'd survived a near-death experience together.

Shit like that tended to bond guys.

"Four years is a long time, Sawyer, and shit, Clint and I, we were just in the beginning of things when he left. I don't know what would've happened if he'd walked in after that long. Hell, I wanted to kill him for staying away from me and it hadn't been nearly that long."

"Yeah, yours was all love at first sight. Rex had a four-year relationship before being away from Josh for four years. And fuck it all, I don't want to be a whiny bitch about it. I get it—all of it. It's just that Rex is the worst, trying to pretend things are normal for us, and they're so far from it."

"Normal's boring," Jace said with a shrug, and Sawyer just stared at him. "What? Dude, I'm not Oprah."

From the other room, they heard Clint howl with laughter.

"I'm glad you're getting enjoyment from my pain, you asshole," Sawyer yelled, then turned to Jace. "You watch Oprah?"

"She doesn't have the daily talk show anymore."

"And the fact that you know that proves my point."

Sawyer continued through his workout, he and Jace focusing on the tasks at hand, which included mentally running through the following day's maneuvers. This planning was where he excelled. He could provide a sniper's plan at a moment's notice, but he could also strategize long-range plans too. And, as Jace pointed out to him yesterday, others were starting to notice.

Yeah, Sawyer had always committed himself to his job, but since hooking up with Rex, he'd thrown himself into it even further. No one was going to ever accuse him of getting preferential treatment because of whom he slept with.

Not that anyone beyond Jace knew who he was sleeping with. But hell, when Sawyer committed to something, it was with his entire heart and soul. And there weren't too many things—or people in his life—he could say that about.

And one of them was currently helping him deal with his shit. Or he had been, until he sat on a bench and stared into space for ten minutes.

Finally, Sawyer put his free weights down and asked, "Who's on your couch today, Oprah?"

"Not funny. And she didn't always use a couch." Jace propped his chin on his hand. "I'm just thinking about Josh. I mean, fuck, if that was one of us...I just can't get it out of my head."

"I know. It's like, what would it take to turn someone. We're so trained but you can't really train for shit like that. Like what happened to us," Sawyer said.

"Couldn't have predicted what we'd do. Couldn't have predicted I wouldn't have killed you and used your body as a floatation device," Jace told him.

"Dude, you're so lucky your secret's already out or I'd be sharing it for you right now."

"Right back at you, brother."

Since both of their secrets revolved around the men they were currently with, it was all good. Six months ago, Sawyer didn't have Rex. Now, he did. If Josh coming back was going to change that, well, then Rex had never really been his to begin with.

Which is pretty much what you've been worrying about.

"You almost killed yourself again. Think we're done for the day," Jace said. "Yeah, you're right."

"Done working. Not done drinking," Jace added, and yes, that was what best friends were for.

6

Dash wasn't in bed with him when he woke up. Lucky's head throbbed, and he just lay there for a long few moments, wishing someone would bring him coffee or aspirin or the like.

Something wasn't right. Hadn't been since Nate had shown up and, while Dash had been able to fuck away Lucky's continuing anxiety yesterday, then last night and well into this morning, the tenseness was back.

Lucky hadn't seen Nate again since the night before last, but he still couldn't shake the feeling of being watched.

He forced himself up and into the living room, where there was still no sign of Dash. He went to the kitchen and drank the juice from the carton as he looked out the side window. Saw Dash standing there, talking to someone. He couldn't see a face, and it could've been anyone. But it made Lucky pause and wait and watch…and finally, the other man moved and it *was* Nate.

Dash was talking to him and Nate was talking with his hands and Lucky had the strangest urge to go out and defend Dash, who didn't look like he needed defending at all.

The first night they'd spent together, he'd told Dash the real story of his missing memories. Dash had listened, then fucked him again, and Lucky had slept better than he had in a long time. And then Dash had hung out with him and Emme—and Emme kept looking between the two of them and smiling—and then she'd given Lucky the afternoon and night off from the bar.

He hadn't argued. It had gone by too damned fast, but he didn't remember feeling that comfortable with anyone since…well, not since he could actually remember anything. He didn't think he'd ever be capable of feeling something, and then Dash had walked in and blown him out of the water.

And now, Dash was talking with the man who could ruin Lucky's pieced-together life.

Dash was your shield from Nate.

But he wouldn't have been forever, though, and Lucky knew that.

Instead of calling down to Dash, he went into the shower, heard the knocking after he turned the water off. He didn't think Dash would continue to knock now that he was staying here, and because they'd fucked, but Lucky didn't know the guy at all.

With the towel wrapped around his waist, he opened the door saying, "After all, you'd think you'd have keys," but for the second time in as many days, a man stood staring at him like he was looking at a ghost.

Because he probably was.

"Sorry. Not who I was expecting." Lucky kept his voice neutral but in his mind that was running a hundred miles an hour, he was packing and leaving. Had to. There wasn't a choice.

"Jesus Christ. Josh." The man's voice broke a little and Lucky stared at him, wishing a memory would come. Because otherwise, he was just a dick standing here coldly, staring at a guy who was clearly emotional.

"I'm Lucky," he said automatically.

"Damned right you are. Shit." A hand went over the guy's shaved head. "I know you spoke to Nate."

"I'm not the guy you want me to be."

"Yeah, you are. Always were. Look, I've got pictures. Please...can I just come in and show them to you? I just need to you know that Nate and I are telling the truth. We lost you for four years. You have no idea..."

He trailed off and Lucky opened the door wider. "I'm just going to get dressed."

The man nodded. Stuck out his hand. "I'm Rex."

Lucky took it in his and stared for a long second, then let go. He turned and left Rex to walk in, and he went into his room and pulled on jeans and a shirt. Thought about making a break for it. But at the very least, he owed Emme and her parents more than that.

Probably owed himself too.

Finally, he went back out to the living room. It was barely noon but he slid into the kitchen and came back with a couple of beers.

Rex took a long pull on his. The guy was handsome. Nervous as Lucky, or maybe more so.

There was a folder on the coffee table. "What's in there?"

"Our past," Rex said and something in his voice made Lucky start.

"We… Nate said we were in the military together."

Rex looked relieved that Lucky was acquiescing. "That too."

Unable to stop his hands from trembling—there wasn't enough beer in the world for that—Lucky slid the pictures out of the manila envelope.

The first were four men, dressed like soldiers. When he noted that, Rex corrected, "Sailors, not soldiers. Navy SEALs, specifically."

"Guess I was a good swimmer."

"The best."

There he was, in between Nate and Rex. Wearing the uniforms. Dog tags. Smiling.

"That's Uncle. Terry Bast. We call him Uncle."

"He's…?"

"Alive, yes."

The next picture was far more surprising. Him with Rex. Dressed in casual clothes. Smiling. Rex's arm slung around him easily. Possessively.

The next photo was almost the same pose, except Lucky was facing Rex.

The next, they were kissing.

"We were…"

"Together. For four years."

"Not me. You were with Josh. I'm not Josh anymore. Maybe I was, but he's long gone. And judging by what I went through, why the hell would I want him to come back?"

The way Rex looked at him was sadness mixed with anger. Maybe pity too. "You don't remember. You really don't."

Lucky shook his head. "You should just go, okay? I'm sorry. And I hope you're happy. That you found someone else, but…"

"You've got to come back with us," Rex said gently. There was a calm command in his voice that made Lucky still.

"Back?"

"The Navy…you're still a part of the Navy. Technically, you'd be up on Desertion charges, but if you really don't have your memories, you'd be considered UA—Unauthorized Absence. I spoke to a JAG who's a friend and he said—"

"Back to the Navy? You've got to be fucking kidding me."

"I'm not." Rex stared at him. "I'm not giving you a chance to run. I owe that to you.

Maybe you don't see it now, but…"

"Fuck you." He shuddered the words out because he was afraid he'd sob if he didn't curse. He swallowed the tears and asked, "Did it ever occur to you that I might not be Josh?"

"Yes. But Dash ran your prints."

"Dash did that?"

The betrayal must've shown clearly on Lucky's face, and he could barely stand the look of pity on Rex's. "I don't understand. Did he know I was there or something?"

"He was following Nate."

"Why's that?"

"That's what you'll find out eventually. But we're not allowed to talk about that. It was the only way the Navy would agree to let me come in here in the first place, or let us escort you home. To the States. Virginia, to be exact."

"The Navy's here?"

"There are two MPs outside, waiting to make sure we get you on the plane."

"Is Dash with the Navy?"

"I don't know. He's definitely not a civilian."

And he hadn't been defending him against Nate at all. He'd been planning with him, waiting, to make sure Lucky didn't leave. He'd known Rex was coming.

He'd known Lucky would be leaving South Africa today, and that he might not ever be able to come back.

"I'm sorry, Lucky. It must be hard not knowing who to trust. But you can trust me. You always did. And the three of us, your team, we'll take you back."

Three men he'd lived and died with would escort him.

Three men determined to yank Josh out of the grave and resurrect him.

Lucky packed while Rex, Nate and Uncle—and the MPs—waited outside, like they were guarding him.

Because they are.

The urge to fight was strong—he recognized it, the same way he'd thought about breaking out of the hospital the night he'd been found on the beach. The same urge had been there that night he'd first seen Nate.

He was capable of fighting. And winning. And because he knew that somewhere deep inside him, he kept his anger tamped down when he found out that Dash had betrayed him.

He kept it in check purposely, because he didn't know exactly what else he was capable of. But he'd done some research on SEALs after texting Emme and asking her to come see him. He wanted to explain things to her himself, and the MPs agreed to let that happen.

He'd done the research in the desperate hope of triggering a memory—any memory. But there was still nothing. He'd also researched the FBI and CIA. He was pretty sure Dash was the latter. Why else would he be involved in this, especially if he wasn't Navy?

Why the hell would he care who Lucky was if he wasn't Navy?

As always, there were more questions than answers.

The bar was open for the afternoon beach crowd, and the music began to drum up under his feet. He sat on the floor, the way he'd done countless times before, and let the music soak over him. Stared up at Dash's framed photographs that lined the walls of the bedroom, like he'd been doing for years and realized that, as a SEAL, he must've worked in some of these areas.

He stood like a shot at that thought. No memories but hell…was that why he'd been so drawn to the photographs? Why he'd taken such comfort from them?

He ran his hands over one of them. Tried to picture Dash taking all of them, trying to rectify the man who'd saved him from Nate, the one who'd given him amazing sex with the man who'd turned him in to Nate and Rex. And the Navy.

"Lucky?" Emme called. He heard male voices mingled in, looked out the bedroom and saw Dash coming into the apartment with her.

Last person he wanted to see.

"You're packing?" she asked.

He couldn't take his eyes from Dash's, wondered when the hell the guy would have the guts to admit what he'd done. "I know you turned me in. What I can't figure out is why you didn't tell me?"

Dash didn't answer, and Lucky was prepared to wait him out.

Emme, of course, wasn't. She looked between him and her brother. "What do you mean, turned you in? Are you running from the law?"

"From the Navy," Dash said, never taking his eyes off Lucky.

"You're a deserter?" Emme asked him.

"He didn't know," Dash said. "Technically, that would make him UA—Unauthorized Absence."

"How gallant, making excuses for me," Lucky told him. "And if you believe that, why the hell didn't you just leave it alone?"

Dash's expression softened for a fleeting second. "No one should be forced to live a lie. Figure out who you are, and then if you want to come back, you come back."

"Why are you making him go, Dash?" Emme asked, stopping Lucky from spitting more angry words at him. "If he has no memory…"

"You knew?" Lucky asked, dragging his eyes from Dash's. Her blue eyes were darker than Dash's, her hair just as blond. She was so pretty. So good to him. And she'd known he'd been lying to her all this time.

"I did," she admitted. "Your story was good. But the way you arrived…the doctor said the scars were fresh."

"You knew and you didn't care that I lied to you?"

"I figured you had your reasons. And you're a good guy, Luck—that much I knew, and that's all that mattered. I'm sorry. Maybe I should've said something."

"Not your fault, Em. You helped me. Saved me. I won't forget that."

"Do what Dash says—figure it out then come back here."

He hugged her and tried to pretend he didn't feel like it was the last time he'd see her.

"Mom and Dad are going to be upset," she said, and he saw her glare at Dash.

"Sorry I couldn't say thanks or goodbye to them."

Emme turned her attention back to Lucky. "Well, call as soon as you can. Tell us where we can find you."

"Yeah."

"Why don't I believe you? Don't make me hunt you down. You know I will."

He knew. "I'll call when I can. Not sure what's going to happen."

She was looking over his shoulder. He turned and saw Nate, Rex and the other man from the photo.

The word *Uncle* couldn't get any more ironic.

"They're arresting you?" Emme asked.

Rex came forward. "Escorting him home safely, ma'am, like we weren't able to do before."

Lucky turned back to her. "They're my team. They were with me...thought I died."

And I did.

"Oh, Lucky." She put a hand on his cheek. "I'm so sorry, for all of you."

"I'll be fine," Lucky told her, which was the biggest lie ever. He didn't know about the rest of them. He glanced at Dash and then back at Rex. "Ready."

Rex grabbed his bag before he could. "I can do that."

"I know. Fuck, I left you behind once. Let me at least carry this for you."

Lucky swallowed a lump in his throat, and he didn't fully understand why he'd gotten choked up to begin with.

Dash got Lucky and his team to the private military plane that awaited them, complete with MPs and JAGs to make sure all of this was by the book.

Lucky turned to him before he boarded the plane, stared at him with a look Dash couldn't place.

It was probably hatred, and Dash could understand that…but a part of him, the wishful-thinking part, thought it was more than that. And then Lucky turned and got on the plane and his team followed.

Dash left the airport before they went wheels-up, spoke to his supervisor as he drove back to talk to Emme, who was no doubt furious with him.

"We'll have to interview your family—you realize that," his supervisor told him. "The CIA and the Navy both want a piece of this."

He'd figured as much, which was why he wasn't on the flight with Lucky.

His supervisor continued, "I think you might have to let them know everything now. You know I don't say that lightly."

Dash had been thinking that as well, all of it. His job depended on secrecy, as did the lives of his family. Shielded for their own good.

Now, all that was going to change. But he couldn't leave them open to danger. "I'll talk to them. They'll cooperate fully."

"And we'll put a team on them until this is straightened out. Your pick."

That would help, but it wasn't perfect. Dash would also call in some private contractors who knew the area well to supplement the CIA. The more the merrier or some shit like that.

"Once that's set up, we need you in Virginia to oversee what's happening with Josh Kent."

He'd been planning on it, but not officially. He didn't want official and Lucky in the same sentence. "I got him there—job over."

"No, it's not."

"It was never an official mission."

"No. But I told you to go with your gut. You were right. You can't just end it here. You can't tell me you want to."

Dash couldn't tell him that. He should want to end things, but what he'd actually thought about was taking Lucky and running with him, bringing him someplace where he could test his memories.

Maybe he was going soft. Maybe he should retire.

Or maybe he'd fallen for someone for the first goddamned time in his life. "He's got amnesia."

"Or he's an excellent liar. Trained, just like you."

Dash winced internally at his supervisor's words. "The shrink can parse that out."

"With your help."

"How?"

"Any way you can, Dashiell. I know how far you'll go for the job. So go there."

Dash couldn't argue, so he didn't.

Emme was waiting for him in the kitchen. Her eyes were red-rimmed and she was tapping the table like she always did, right before she exploded.

She stared up at him. Didn't say anything. And that wasn't like her at all.

"I'm really sorry," he started.

"Who are you?" she asked. "What's your job, Dashiell?"

It could only be worse if she middle-named him. "I'm with the CIA."

She stared. Blinked. Shook her head and muttered to herself and then pointed at him. Said nothing. Pointed again, then put her hands together on the table.

"I tried to shield you from this shit forever, Em. Didn't want you to worry."

She turned to him. She looked stunned, rightfully so, and no doubt angry and scared, and it was everything he hadn't wanted to do to her.

"I'm sorry, Em," he said quietly.

"You're a CIA agent."

"Yes."

"Like on TV."

"They don't always get it right," he offered lamely, and when she glared he nodded. "Yes, like that."

"And you came here to find Lucky."

"No. That was…coincidence. I was following Nate, the SEAL from his team."

"You think he was coming here to hurt us?"

"He said he was coming here to surf. He seemed as surprised to find Lucky here as I was."

"And you think Lucky was sent here to hurt us but lost his memory instead?"

"I don't know. That's what I'm trying to find out."

"I need some time," she said quietly, her arms wrapped around herself. "I need to just take some time and absorb all ofthis."

"Look, I get that, but we have to talk first," he said.

"About Lucky?"

"Yes."

She dropped her arms to her sides and slumped into

the kitchen chair. Their parents wouldn't be back until that evening—he wouldn't leave her alone until then.

Nate had seemed surprised that Lucky was living with Dash's family, but they were all skillfully trained liars, and Dash was trained to not believe anyone.

And yet, he believed Lucky. So fuck his training to hell.

"What do you want to know?" she asked.

"Hate to say it, but can you start from the beginning?"

She did, told him the story of finding Lucky, her tone flat the entire time, a monotone monologue. Everything she said matched Lucky's timeline to a T. She talked about how balanced the books were since he got here. How he split his tips because he said he didn't need anything. She told him that the majority of the tips were Lucky's, which Dash could easily see. She talked about his demeanor. His general habits.

Dash had already swept the apartment, house and bar and found nothing out of the ordinary. "Relationships?"

"One-night stands. He was lonely, but he wouldn't let himself get involved." She sounded so defensive.

"Did he ever meet with anyone who made you feel uncomfortable?"

"Are you kidding me with this?"

"No, I'm not."

"I never saw any terrorist at the bar."

"This isn't an interrogation."

"Feels like it."

"It's part of my job, Em. I've got to protect you."

"Wouldn't need to if you didn't bring the danger to us." She stared at him like she'd never seen him before. "So what else is a lie?"

"Nothing."

"The photography is."

"No, it's not. That's a separate job that happened to work perfectly with this one. It's what I'd be doing anyway. I'm just lucky I can combine the two."

At the mention of the word *lucky*, she blanched. "When can I talk to him?"

"I really don't know."

"Could the answer be never?"

"I don't want it to be." Truth be told, he'd love to clear these guys. They were American heroes, best of the best.

And if one or all had been turned, it meant they could easily be the worst of the worst.

He turned the empty bottle of Fanta in his hands at the table he'd grown up at.

He'd been sitting here alone when the call had come in. He'd been twenty at the time, home from college in the States for summer break. And the man on the other end of the line had wanted to talk to him about his future.

Dash had dual citizenship—his mom was from the States, dad born and bred in South Africa. Up until Emme went to college, the family had spent part of every year in the States and Dash had gone to college there. He'd been into mixed martial arts. Semi- pro boxing. Knew how to fire weapons. Add the photography to that, and as his future supervisor would tell him on that day, "You're the perfect storm. Everything we look for in an agent."

It happened fast after that. He didn't finish college. Not formally, anyway. His family thought he dropped out of school because he'd gotten the photography job of a lifetime, his big break. And that was partially true.

So he'd built his life from there on out on partial truths.

"If this hadn't happened, when were you going to tell me?" Emme finally asked.

"Never, if I could help it."

She went to walk away and he said, "I know you're pissed, but I never wanted you to have to live the life I did."

"That wasn't your choice to make. You made it for all of us."

"Because my job dictates that."

There wasn't going to be a day that went by where Em wouldn't be looking over her shoulder. That built-in superstition would haunt her. Would affect the rest of her life.

"When will we know if we're out of danger?"

He didn't tell her that he'd been given the option to relocate them, that if it were solely up to him, he'd pack his family up and get them the hell out of there.

But they'd never leave. And he wouldn't force that. He would, however, hire guards that would double as bouncers, put in extra security and the like, in addition to the CIA team that would be guarding his family until this Lucky-slash-Josh situation was figured out.

And then he'd head to Virginia and figure out what the hell Josh was up to.

"You slept with him," Emme said now. "Was that part of the job?"

How could he tell her the answer to that was both yes and no? The most honest answer tumbled out of his mouth before he could stop it. "I like him."

Emme leaned against the door. "Like as in, want a relationship? Are those allowed in your job?"

He snorted. "They're not encouraged, and he's the first guy I've liked in a long time."

"And he might be here to hurt us."

He shrugged.

"You consider yourself a good judge of character, right, Dash? Do you think you could fall for someone who might hurt us?"

"They say love's blind, right?"

"Ah, Dash." She went and hugged him. "He's perfect for you."

"That's why you let him stay?"

"We let him stay because we think he's a good person. You won't get me to believe otherwise. I mean, he's had a million chances to hurt us. It's not like he asked questions about you. He never went in your room in the apartment.

He refused. He was the one who saved Dad's life when he had the heart attack two years ago. He came to us broken, needing family, and he found it. We love him." She sighed. "This is going to crush Mom and Dad."

And it did. When his parents heard what happened—from Emme, of course—they were furious. At Dash. Probably because Emme added in the fact that he'd slept with Lucky, when he hadn't actually confirmed that, and now they were like the morality police.

The disappointment on his father's face was the hardest to bear, and it had nothing to do with what Dash had done to Lucky.

Everyone was upset that Dash hadn't trusted them. What Dash didn't bother to tell them was that this time he didn't even trust himself.

7

Sawyer couldn't sit still. A long run down the beach did shit to tamp down the tension that continued to rattle his body with every pounding step in the wet sand.

He ran until he couldn't any longer, and since he'd had to run for his life on several occasions, that was a hell of a long time. But even though his body shut off, his mind refused to.

He imagined that's what it must've been like for Rex in that prison, when he'd been captured. Imagined what it would be like to see someone you thought had died step in front of you.

Imagined how much things in his future could change because of this.

When he got back, he took a long, hot shower. His body had turned to mush but his mind would never let him sleep. He planned on settling in with several action-packed movies in the hopes they'd at least keep his mind entertained when the phone rang.

He'd figured it'd be Jace, who'd tried to get him to hang

out with him and Clint again. But drinking hadn't helped anything. Rex had warned Sawyer about the radio silence, but when he said, "Hey," and Rex's voice answered, "Did I wake you?" Sawyer fucking melted.

"I've been worried about you," he admitted before he could stop himself.

"I've been worried about you," Rex countered.

He couldn't even ask Rex where he was. Realized that Rex might be on base and couldn't tell him. "Have you been sleeping at all?"

"Always have trouble without you next to me. In case you hadn't noticed, my sleep patterns have vastly improved with you in my bed."

"I noticed," he said quietly. Rex had to be someplace private if he was able to talk about things like that, so he breathed a little easier. Things were okay.

"Good. Because I assumed you did, but then I realized that I should probably stop assuming and start telling you."

"Thanks." Sawyer closed his eyes, said a silent prayer that he'd say the right thing. "Is Josh okay?"

"He's alive. He's okay."

He let out a long breath. "Good."

"He looks the same. Like time stood still for him. And he doesn't remember anything. Not me or his time with the teams. Or anything before four years ago."

Sawyer didn't know what to say. Figured Rex just needed for him to listen but he couldn't help but add, "I'm glad he has you there."

There was a long pause. "You're a special one, Sawyer."

"Is—"

"I don't want to talk about it anymore. Not right now. Things are strange and crazy, but I couldn't sleep because I was thinking about you. No one else but you. This conversation's about you from this point onward."

Sawyer's cock got hard at the tone and the implication of Rex's words. He'd automatically headed to the bedroom, collapsed on the sheets that smelled like Rex.

Rex had asked him to stay here while he was gone, asked that Sawyer be here when he got back. Sawyer hadn't had the heart to refuse and now was glad he hadn't.

"Get yourself comfortable, baby," Rex purred. "But first, grab the laptop. Want to see you."

Sawyer smiled and grabbed for the MacBook Air on the night table. He turned on Skype and waited for it to load as he got naked.

Rex looked tired but his eyes were bright. Sawyer put a finger up to the computer as if to touch his face.

"This is nice," Rex said. "Wanted to see your face when you came."

"You're coming too," he replied and Rex snorted.

"Someone's feeling his oats."

"Damned straight."

Sawyer lay on his side, lubed his cock and began to stroke it the way Rex told him to, first long and slow and then fast and hard until he was begging Rex to let himcome.

"More than once," Rex said. "Love to hear you beg."

"I want you inside me. Fuck, if I think hard enough, I can feel your cock in my ass."

"Jesus, Sawyer." The bed on Rex's side rustled and he knew, just by the sound of the man's voice, that Rex was jerking off. "Want to bend you over the nearest couch. Or my desk. Wouldn't care where you were or who was around when I did it. I'd hold you down, bite the back of your neck. Drive into you until you were yelling my name. Because I love it when you yell my name."

"Yeah, I'd do that. Fucking take everything you gave me."

Their relationship had started out with phone sex, because that had been the most non-threatening for Sawyer.

He still liked the memories it brought back, and the orgasm raced through him. Rex shouted softly as he came a minute later. But Sawyer couldn't find that good, contented feeling he usually had when an orgasm abated.

Rex, of course, noticed. "Trouble staying still?"

"I am still."

Rex frowned and Sawyer realized his foot was shaking, which in turn made his entire body shake. It was such a part of his constant need for motion that it rarely registered with him anymore. And it turned itself off in high-danger situations, like a survival switch. "I guess I just need to come again."

"I won't let you come unless you stop moving."

"Guess I'm never coming then." Frustrated, he let go of his cock.

"Want to tell me what's going on? Besides the obvious?"

"It's my mind, Rex. I'm comfortable. I'm relaxed. I just can't shut my mind off," he said.

"Talk to me, baby."

"It's not the time."

"It's always the time to tell me how you're feeling. Please," Rex added, and Sawyer blurted out, "I feel like we don't know each other outside of work."

"Work is us, Sawyer. Work does define us. It's not a typical job."

"You think because you see me at work that you know everything about me?"

"Not everything. But discovering's a big part of the fun."

Sawyer leaned back against the pillows. "That's true."

"So what don't you know about me?"

"If I don't know it, how do I know what I don't know?" Sawyer asked, and Rex laughed. "Okay, start with the Dom stuff."

"What about it?"

"I know you were really into it at one point. And then, not so much."

"I was, before Josh. And then I went so far opposite of it and I felt lost. Until I found you, and then I found myself again. Does that make sense?"

"Yeah, it does."

"I don't want to be a full-time Dom with you, Sawyer. You'd hate that. But I do know how to calm you when you can't calm yourself. I'll show you that I can fix it, if you'll let me."

"How can you do that?"

"Next time I see you in person, I'll show you."

"And for now?"

"We're back in that shower, the night you were watching me," Rex started, and Sawyer's entire body flooded with heat again. "I'm jacking myself off, and you think you're safe. Hidden. You watch me come and then you go back to your bunk. You're alone in there, because the rest of the guys are out on watch. You're supposed to be getting shut-eye, so you lie down and close your eyes."

Sawyer's hand snaked around his cock, but he didn't stroke himself for fear he'd come and end the story.

"I pull the covers off you, and you try to get up, but I've got surprise on my side. I tie you, facedown, to your bunk. Spread-eagled. And you're begging me to let you go. But I won't, not until you tell me to fuck you."

"Fuck me," Sawyer breathed without thinking.

"Good boy. Because if you didn't agree, I told you I'd leave you there, just like this, for the other men to see. That's not to say they won't come in and find me fucking you though."

A groan escaped. Sawyer loved these fantasies, because they were safe. Because Rex told him time and time again he had no interest in sharing him or risking his career like that.

But as a fantasy…hot as hell.

"I'm running a finger down your ass. I'm asking you if you've ever done this before.

You tell me no. I tell you this is what you get when you spy on your CO."

"Couldn't help it. You looked so hot. You knew I was there the whole fucking time, too." He hadn't known at the time, but knowing it now made the whole thing that much sweeter to revisit.

"I'm going to eat your ass, Sawyer, because you love it and because you're embarrassed at how much you love it still," Rex said, his drawl deepening and yeah, that was true. Sawyer's face flushed as soon as he said the words and he began to stroke his cock, his hips rocking back and forth as he imagined Rex's tongue doing all those things that made Sawyer go completely fucking wild.

He came with a huge shudder, kept his eyes on Rex's the entire time. Loved it that the man came immediately after he did.

"It's probably the last time I can talk to you like this for a while."

"Why's that?"

"I've been talking to the JAG. There are questions for me and Nate and Uncle. It's going to be fine, but we're going to have to sort things out. No different than being sent on a mission," Rex said quietly, and they both let the lie slide.

They fell asleep with only the computer screen between them. Sawyer woke up multiple times during the night, only to find Rex still there. Not sleeping, but each time, nodding to let Sawyer know he was still there.

He's still there.

8

Lucky slept on and off for the last leg of the plane ride to Virginia and the naval base he'd been told he'd been a part of for years.

He didn't even remember living in Virginia. Didn't remember what state he'd been born in, grown up in. Didn't know if anyone would truly believe that.

Dash does.

And Dash also sold him down the river. So maybe Lucky no longer knew when someone was bullshitting him.

He deplaned, followed by Rex, Uncle and Nate. Rex still carried his bag, but that was taken from him once they entered the main building. Lucky was being treated with a mixture of respect and suspicion, sometimes both at the same time, and it was beginning to freak him the fuck out.

It had happened during the stopover before the States, but not to this extreme. He'd been treated and checked for diseases—that was all the doctors would tell him—and he knew he'd have to undergo more extensive exams once he reached Virginia.

But now that he was here, he was given extra escorts into the building. Men in uniform who surrounded him like he was a bomb they were worried would detonate.

Am I?

He went through a metal detector and then he was wanded. As a final security measure, he was asked to take his shirt off.

They all were, so he didn't feel so set apart. He noted the scars on all three men's backs, identical to his, and his throat tightened.

He looked away, pulled his shirt back on and waited for his next directive. None came immediately, so he moved closer to Rex and Uncle and Nate.

"What the hell?" he asked Rex, whose face was unreadable. Rex glanced at Nate and Uncle, both of whom nodded.

"They're worried about your abilities."

"Like, psychic abilities? Did I forget I have those too?" Lucky asked, and Nate snorted.

"Same old Josh," he mumbled, but there was a smile on his face. For that reason alone, Lucky's nerves calmed. Until Rex continued, "You're a weapon. You don't remember your training or what you can do…"

"But when you came after me in the parking lot, I knew," Nate added.

"Have you fought with anyone in the past years? I mean, an honest to-God fight?" Uncle asked, a hesitation in his voice.

Lucky shook his head. "I bounced at the bar, but the furthest I had to go was dragging guys out or breaking fights up. I never became part of them."

Rex nodded. "Makes sense. You've got that presence."

Lucky wouldn't have known what the hell he was talking about a month ago, but in the short time he'd spent with the men who'd been his team, he understood. Even retired, Nate and Uncle weren't guys you fucked with—one look and you just knew to give them a wide berth. It was magnified with Rex. But the fact that they felt Lucky himself gave off that vibe, well, that shocked the hell out of him.

It made things more understandable to him, however, when there was the brief discussion as to whether he should be handcuffed during his physical after a ride in the elevator with two MPs flanking him.

Rex looked at Lucky and then at the doctor waiting and said, "I think he'll be fine."

Lucky couldn't be as sure, but he didn't want to be both handcuffed and pawed at unless there was an orgasm attached to the end of the experience. This didn't look promising, as the doctor was maybe seventy and decidedly not gay, but at least he looked friendly.

Scratch that—he didn't look terrified at the thought of spending time alone with a trained killer with amnesia. Lucky moved past him into the exam room, and the doctor shut the door quietly.

Everything he did was quiet and controlled.

"I'm Dr. Larkin. I'm going to be examining you today."

"I'm Lucky."

Dr. Larkin nodded and picked up the file from the countertop.

"I mean, I know the file doesn't say that's my name, but that's what I go by."

Dr. Larkin looked through the file for a few moments before saying, "Your name's Josiah. But it looks like everyone called you Josh. I'm guessing you always went by it."

He tried both names out on his tongue but nothing pinged in his brain. He shook his head, frustrated, and the doctor stared at him.

"Okay, I'll just call you Lucky then, for now," he said quietly.

"Thanks." He stared down at his hands balled in his lap. "Are they sending me to jail?"

"I hope not. But a JAG will be around to talk to you."

"They were on the plane with me but they told me to keep my mouth shut, not to even ask questions." And he hadn't.

"Let's get through your medical reviews, okay? If you have nothing to hide, none of this should be a problem."

Maybe that was wishful thinking, but Lucky wanted to believe it more than anything.

Dr. Larkin put the file down and said, "I'd like to give you privacy to undress, but I can't. So I'll get ready while you strip down. Put the gown on, opening in the front."

Lucky stared at it. "Seriously? Isn't it easier to go naked?"

"They have rules about these things for doctors."

Dr. Larkin had some snark going and Lucky decided he liked the guy. So he stripped and put the gown on while the doctor washed up and lined up his instruments.

"Do you have any issues with touch or sound?" he asked before he started.

"I don't know what you mean."

"Do loud noises startle you more than you think they should? Are you hyperaware of noise, or when someone puts a hand on you? If I came up to you from behind and put a hand on your shoulder, would you react violently without thinking about it?"

Lucky just stared at him, the questions mixing up in his mind. "I don't...no one's ever really tried that."

Dr. Larkin smiled a little. "I can see why. I won't make any moves without telling you what I'm doing first. Fair enough?"

"Sure."

The exam was standard doctor stuff except for the photographs he took of Lucky's scarring. He asked about Lucky's aches and pains, told him not to be a tough guy but to answer truthfully.

"The scars pull. My back and thighs ache more than they should from just scars. Other than that...you know, beyond the fact that I can't remember anything before four years ago, I'm great."

"The scars are deep. Lots of trauma to the muscle, which is why you'll have the pain.

If you need something stronger than ibuprofen, I can write you a prescription."

"No thanks."

"What about sleeping?"

"That's not a problem."

"Nightmares?"

He stared at the doctor, flashing back to his talk with Dash. "I don't dream."

"Interesting. I'm going to set up a CT scan and an MRI for you. See what we can find out. Any seizures?"

"No."

"Good. Headaches? Blurry vision?"

"No."

After ticking off the doctor's laundry list of items and finding out he was in damned good shape, Dr. Larkin closed the file. "Do you have any questions for me?"

"Can I see those?" he asked, pointed to the photos on the counter. Dr. Larkin looked reluctant for a second before handing over the Polaroids.

"Do you want to see the psychiatrist before you do that?" he asked.

"You think I'm going to freak out?"

"You might. Any drug allergies?"

"Not that I know of."

He stared down at the pictures. He'd seen the scars in the mirror, of course, or at least as much of them as he could. But the photographs were different. It was like he was looking at a stranger."Fuck."

"Lucky, what's wrong?"

"It's just...I didn't know they were this bad." He rarely went shirtless, and when he did at the beach, he was always aware of the whispers behind his back. The scars on his legs only reached to right above his knees, so they were hidden. But they were thick and roped. "Why didn't they heal?"

The doctor was silent for a long moment. "You're not supposed to tell me anything,right?"

"Right." He turned around and then handed Lucky the file. "I suppose letting you read isn't the same as telling you."

Lucky took the file and stared at it, and then he handed it back to the doc. "I'm not ready."

Dr. Larkin took it back. "They put salt in the wounds— literally—to make sure they scarred. It would make things more painful for you, both then and now."

Unconsciously, he reached up to rub one of them on his shoulder that always seemed to pull when he got tired. Dr. Larkin smiled at him, a real smile.

"I think you're going to be fine, Lucky. I think you deserve that."

"Thanks, Doc."

"Just wait here while I call for your escort. Not sure if you can go straight to the scans or if they have other plans foryou."

Rex came in past the doctor. "Everything okay?"

"Healthy as a horse." He paused. "The doctor was nice to me. It's like they're scared of me, but they're nice."

"You're a decorated SEAL. You were awarded a posthumous Purple Heart," Rex told him. "I guess we can cross out the posthumous part."

"Won't they take it away?"

"Why? Just because you don't remember what you did doesn't mean it didn't happen. I was there—I was by your side for just about every mission you ever did with the SEALs, including that last one. You more than goddamned deserve it. You deserve a hell of a lot more."

9

"Sawyer, it's your mother."

"Hey, Mom." He clutched the cell phone hard enough to leave dents in his hands. He dropped it to the table, put it on speakerphone and asked, "Where are you?"

Because she mainly called when she was close to Virginia, like she knew he couldn't escape.

"I'm in Virginia, visiting some friends. Tonight, I'm going to the Scanlons' party. Remember, I sent you the invitation last month?"

"Vaguely, but I've been away a lot…"

"And you told me you could go."

"I don't ever remember saying that."

"I RSVP'd to the Scanlons for you."

"Shit."

"Sawyer, language. I'm not in the Navy." His mother sighed. "Tonight at ten. I'm resending the invitation right now. Oh, and they'd like you to bring some of your friends."

"Why's that?"

"They want a nice showing of active-duty military. Wear

your dress whites. Can't wait to see you."

She hung up before he could say anything. Damn, she was good.

He checked his email, found the invitation and stared at it for a few minutes. He couldn't get out of going—and he'd drag Jace along. Rex wasn't supposed to be back until... well, hell, he wasn't exactly clued in to the details, for security purposes.

He looked down at his phone and saw his friend trying to Face Chat with him. He pulled up the app and saw Jace sitting on the couch. "Want to go out tonight?"

"I have to go out tonight and you're coming with me. My mom's in town."

"I'm not great with mothers."

"You don't have to do anything but go to this party. She wants me to bring other uniforms. Wants heroes."

Clint walked behind the couch where Jace was sitting and gave Sawyer a wave as Jace said, "So I'm like your date."

"Keep being an asshole—see where that gets you."

Jace pointed at Clint's retreating back. "I was an asshole to him sometimes and it got me..."

"I can hear you," Clint called over his shoulder. "Go with Sawyer to the party. Make connections. It's good for both of your careers."

Six hours later, dressed in their dress whites and ribbons, Sawyer and Jace entered the grand ballroom that was already crowded with socialites and a few members of the press. A woman came up to them, checked their names off a list and asked them if they preferred not to have their pictures taken.

"No ma'am, we'd rather not," Sawyer told her.

"Certainly." She walked away and spoke to the man with the camera. When she came back, she told them, "It's been noted. If you show up on the video, your faces will be blurred. Also, your medals."

"Thank you."

"Thank you both. Please enjoy the party."

"How'd you swing an invite to this?" Jace asked when she was out of hearing.

"I told you my mom's in town—she forced this on me and I forced it on you, because that's what friends are for."

Jace snorted, then said, "Your mom runs in these circles? Why am I just hearing about that?"

Sawyer shrugged.

"This is like, *this is your life, Sawyer Thomas.*"

"Sawyer Kirke Thomas."

Jace's eyes widened. "You've got to be kidding me."

"Wish I was."

"Boy, you've got some explaining to do."

"Couldn't talk about everything when we were in that cave," Sawyer shot back.

Jace stared at him and then looked around the party. "You hated it, didn't you? Growing up in this life."

"Yeah," he admitted quietly.

Jace put a hand on his shoulder. "You're free, Sawyer. This is just a visit. And I'm going to get us something to drink. Try not to get married to a socialite when I'm gone."

"Funny. You're funny. Can see why Clint keeps you around," he called as Jace walked away. Watched many pairs of eyes follow his friend, because yeah, Jace was as all-American good-looking as they got.

He felt like a weight had been lifted by telling Jace this. He hadn't been hiding it, but you didn't just walk up to people and tell them you were filthy stinking rich.

Now he had to let Rex know about it. Because he'd been bitching to Rex that they didn't know each other while he'd been keeping this secret.

But it had stopped being a secret a long time ago for him. Instead, it became simply a life that he'd felt had never been his. He'd never felt rich. He'd grown up running roughshod over any culture his mother tried to give him. That's not to say he hadn't picked up any social graces. He could hold his own at any fancy party, knew how to make the right kind of small talk to keep people comfortable.

He also knew how to make people decidedly uncomfortable, but that didn't come from practice. That was a skill that he'd been born with, and whether or not he did it with a question or a look, he was always able to suss out both truth and lies.

He was also able to hide his own truth and lies. It helped him to rise up the ranks in the military and he'd been recommended for OCS but hadn't gone.

Rex had been actively trying to talk him into it. Sawyer had been just as actively refusing.

"I work for a living," was an old military joke non-officers used when someone addressed them as *sir* but that wasn't far from the truth for Sawyer.

He could've gone to an elite military academy, just like his father had. Could be working in the Pentagon. Instead, he was happily ensconced in a SEAL team.

Didn't matter how highly decorated he was or how many missions he'd clocked, the lives he'd saved. His mother was proud he'd followed in his father's footsteps but angry that she had to worry about him. It brought back too many memories for her, and it complicated their already complicated relationship further.

At least he didn't have to live with her. That was her new boyfriend's job and hell, if the guy wanted to hang around and play second fiddle, so be it. He'd find out soon enough, like his stepfather had, that there was only one man in his mother's life.

He'd been five when his dad was killed. Didn't remember much, although the memories were good.

And knowing how much his mother still mourned for her first love had been what stopped Sawyer cold when he'd first discovered Rex's boyfriend had been killed. Rex had assured Sawyer that wasn't the case in their relationship and Sawyer had finally gotten comfortable enough to believe it.

But now, the ghost wasn't a ghost any longer.

Love was a powerful, funny thing—the connection was indescribable. And no matter who tried to convince him that Rex didn't see Sawyer as coming in second…well, Sawyer knew how he felt about Rex, knew that the man had changed him in a way he'd never be able to adequately describe or forget.

When someone touched you that deeply, you didn't ever forget it.

Jace handed him a Coke, because he knew Sawyer didn't drink at all when he drove.

Jace had designated him the driver and designated himself the invited guest.

He was drinking a dirty martini. Correction, he drank half and put it down. None of them drank with any regularity these days, so when they did go out to get hammered, it happened pretty quickly. He didn't want that to happen tonight.

"I'm guessing Rex doesn't know about any of this, right?"

"No."

"Does your mom know about Rex?"

"No."

"You're not planning on revealing that shit here, are you? Because I only brought one set of restraints and that could get ugly."

"You brought cuffs? To this? Did you think a brawl would happen or were you planning on randomly arresting people?"

"No, they're for later when I meet Clint."

Sawyer held up a hand. "I don't need to hear any more."

Jace grinned. "Mom alert. She's waving and pointing and mouthing, *my son.*"

Sawyer turned around just in time. His mother was coming toward him, her high heels clipping along the floor.

"Sawyer." She hugged him, then kissed him—no air kisses, which was something he liked. She never did that fake shit.

She hugged Jace too, and he mouthed "Your mom's hot" over her shoulder. She was, but Sawyer mouthed back "Asshole" anyway.

After a few minutes of catch-up and small talk, Mom's newest boyfriend, a retired three-star admiral, came over and introduced himself.

Both Sawyer and Jace saluted and then he shook both their hands. "I appreciate the salute. I know those are rare gifts from SEALs."

It was true—SEALs didn't salute many people. But, like Clint said, this was good for both their careers and it never hurt to give a little respect to a three-star.

He actually seemed like a good guy, which meant that Mom would run him out of town pretty quickly.

Jace was talking to his mom, and the admiral told Sawyer, "It's good to meet you, son. I've heard great things about you from Admiral Beck. He said you're on the fast track for a promotion. That you're one of the best operators he's seen in a long time."

"Thank you, sir."

"Listen son, I heard what happened to your CO."

"Word spreads fast."

"I'm sure the investigation won't prove anything against him," he said, and Sawyer schooled his face and pretended the admiral's words weren't a punch to the gut. Because the admiral was talking about Rex and goddammit, Sawyer had put the fact that Rex could find himself in real trouble out of his head. Because that's the way Rex had wanted it. But if it had gotten this far along the chain, if the admiral was hearing rumors about the investigation…

Sawyer forced himself to stop thinking and just answer, "Yes, sir."

"If there's anything I can do for him, for you, you'll let me know?"

"Yes sir."

"I mean it, Sawyer. Don't be afraid to call in a favor if need be. The Navy's tough on deserters, but the scuttlebutt is that his teammates knew nothing about his deception."

"Ray, let's dance."

His mother put her hand on the admiral's shoulder and led him away to the dance floor. As Sawyer watched, he wondered how much longer she could keep faking it—and she was, because he knew what her real smile looked like.

Jace wandered back over. "I've got five phone numbers."

"Men or women?"

His friend's smile was wicked. "Little of both. The uniform's a fucking magnet."

That was the truth. "You gonna tell Clint?"

"Yeah, because there's nothing much better than Clint when he's jealous." Jace looked around. "Who bothered you?"

"What are you talking about?"

"Seriously? You're going to try to fool me?"

Neither had been able to do that since their near-death experience during a mission. They'd shared a lot when they thought they might not make it. They even made promises to fulfill when they got out.

Since then, they'd been tight as hell. "The admiral mentioned that Rex is being investigated because of Josh. Rex mentioned that he'd be questioned too, but he glossed over it. We both did."

"Maybe the admiral was trying to give you a head's-up that you should pass along to Rex? Maybe Rex can call him for advice?"

"I don't know. Shit. Come on, let's get out of here."

They'd been driving for half an hour when Sawyer glanced in the rearview and said, "We're definitely being followed."

"I knew that twenty minutes ago," Jace said, not taking his eyes from the side-view mirror he'd been staring into for most of the ride home.

Sawyer had known as well, but he'd been hoping he was wrong.

"I'm guessing this isn't a coincidence, then, that everyone knows about Rex and Josh and all that shit?" Jace asked.

"Guessing not."

"Want me to call Clint and see if he knows anything?"

"Talk to him when you get home. Right now, I plan on having a little fun with whoever the asshole following us is."

When Sawyer slammed in, wearing full dress whites, Rex's breath caught in his throat. He looked incredibly handsome. Strong.

He also looked surprised, but the smile came quickly. "Shit, I would've stayed home if I'd known you'd be back tonight. I was…"

He was on Sawyer, kissing him before he could get the rest of the words out. Sawyer's arms wound around him, the kisses messy and wet in no time as they were stripping and trying to move to the bedroom.

They ended up making it to the stairs. Rex pushed Sawyer back and got his pants down. With one leg out, Rex's finger slid inside Sawyer.

Sawyer grunted. "Yeah, more, Rex."

"Let me find lube."

"Don't need it."

"Not going to hurt you," Rex said, stared at Sawyer so he understood the complete truth behind those words. He grabbed lube from a drawer in the den and came back to find Sawyer exactly where he'd left him. Waiting, sprawling lazily, half out of his uniform.

Rex got naked—loved feeling Sawyer's clothes rub his skin. He put one of Sawyer's legs over his shoulder, opened him. Entered him, cock halfway in, watching Sawyer's face flush. His mouth went slack with pleasure—he pushed his hips up to meet Rex's cock and Rex pushed in, up to his balls.

"Yeah, come on, Rex…missed you."

Sawyer grabbed the banister with one hand, Rex's shoulder with the other as Rex drove into him, until it was just their moans and flesh slapping flesh.

Sawyer's leg wrapped around Rex's ass, pulling him closer. Rex put his mouth on Sawyer's and they moaned into each other's mouths.

"Missed you," he muttered against Sawyer's neck. "I think my whole body's asleep."

Rex huffed a laugh. He pushed up and then he grabbed Sawyer, who managed to wrap around him. When they got into bed, he wiped Sawyer down and then himself.

"Why the uniform?"

"Had a function."

"Kind of figured that."

"I guess we both have things we don't want to talk

about," Sawyer said. There wasn't anger in his voice, onlyresignation.

Rex ran a hand through Sawyer's hair, propped on his elbow as he stared down at him. "I'm not trying to keep things from you. But I wanted to be with you tonight. You first. You come first."

Sawyer nodded.

"We turned him over to the Navy. Escorted him here. He's in solitary. Going to get a full work-up."

"He really doesn't remember you?"

"He doesn't remember anything before four years ago."

"I don't know if that's good or bad." Rex didn't answer that because he couldn't, and Sawyer continued with, "I know the Navy's investigating you."

"It's a technicality, Sawyer. I've got to go back tomorrow and I'll probably be gone for a couple of weeks while the JAGs go over shit with me."

"About the mission?"

"Yes. What about you? What don't you want to tell me?"

"It's not that I don't want to. Fuck. It's not a big deal."

"Bullshit," Rex said quietly.

"My mom's in town. That's why I went to the party."

"I know you had a rough time with her." Rex knew that was where a lot of Sawyer's worry about Josh came from. Sawyer had admitted as much when they'd first gotten together. He hadn't wanted to compete with a ghost.

And even though Josh wasn't a ghost anymore, there

was no competition. "How is she?"

"Dating a retired admiral. They wanted some active-duty guys. Good for press. I brought Jace."

"Am I going to get to meet her?"

"I'd rather not go there, Rex. She lives in Europe. I barely see her. The less she knows about my life, the better. I'd feel that way no matter who I was dating."

"Okay, I get that. But what I'm not getting is what you don't want to talk about."

"My mom's last name is Kirke."

Rex stared at the beautiful man in his bed, at his aristocratic features. "As in, Kirke Industries?"

"One and the same."

"Your mom's Jude Kirke."

"I didn't realize you kept up with the socialites."

"She's hard to miss. So your stepfather was Adam Knoll, the actor?"

"Yeah." He looked at Rex. "Thomas is my father's last name. My full name's Sawyer Kirke Thomas, but I never spell it out. Pissed my mom off."

"Are you…"

"Rich? Yes. I've got a shitload of cash. Don't have to work another day. My mother would rather me be sitting on the board and doing charity work. Nothing wrong with that— my family's done a lot of good stuff, but I want—needed— something different."

Rex ran a finger over Sawyer's collarbone. "Are all the

secrets out now?"

Sawyer stared at him. "Are they ever?"

The next morning, Rex was gone by 0400. Sawyer tossed and turned, was up by 0500. Jace and Clint were at his door half an hour later.

"What the hell were you two thinking, losing a tail and not mentioning it to me until morning?" Clint demanded.

"He went home to you." Sawyer pointed to Jace, who went to the mirror and stared into it. "What are you doing?"

"Checking for the tire marks on my face from the bus you just threw me under."

"Don't try to throw me off topic—I invented that shit," Clint informed them.

"Why didn't you tell me that he invented it? We should put his name in Wikipedia," Sawyer said, and Clint shook a finger at him.

"Don't. Unless you want me to call Rex?"

"He's unavailable."

Clint crossed his arms.

"What? He's dealing with the fallout from Josh."

"Just like the admiral said," Clint finished.

"I guess you told him everything," Sawyer said to Jace.

Jace mouthed "Handcuffs" and pointed to Clint from behind his back. "I know what you're saying, Jace."

"Do you think he really knows for sure, or he just knows you well enough to know you might be saying something?" Sawyer asked.

"Doing it again," Clint said, but he was already moving around.

"What're you doing?"

Clint didn't answer—he was under the mantel for a few minutes and then he said, "Someone bugged this house."

"When?"

Clint assessed it. "Recently. This one's maybe a week old."

Sawyer backtracked, his mind going furiously over what it could've picked up.

"Sawyer, this isn't a typical bug. This won't record voice or video. This is more of a tracker. It picks up body heat."

"So they'll know when someone's home or not," Sawyer said slowly.

"There's one under your car too," Jace reported. "Figured we're better off leaving them and not tipping our hand."

Clint agreed. "I'll set up some surveillance of my own."

"This can't be Josh—he's under lockdown," Sawyer said.

"That's right. But it could be the men who captured him. Because he was turned.

Because they want him back, memories or no memories," Clint said, and Jace cursed. "You need to tell Rex," Jace said.

"He's under enough scrutiny right now," Sawyer said.

"And if they found out you hid this, that might make it worse," Clint pointed out. "Did you ever stop to think that maybe Rex is still in danger from the men who captured him? And that maybe you're involved too?"

Sawyer hadn't really considered that. Jace hadn't either, judging by the way he continued cursing. "You think one of those men might've been following us last night?"

Clint sighed. "Could've been CIA. Could've been anyone. But I'm reporting this. And you'll stay with us until Rex comes home again. No arguments."

Rex waited in the room where he'd been meeting with JAGs and other naval officers about the mission he'd been a part of. About the capture and release. About Josh.

His own memories had held up, for the most part. He got the feeling now that this was more about making sure he wasn't in danger.

That was something he'd never really considered, that the terrorist who'd let them go would have further interest in them. Not until one of the JAGs told him that his friend Clint had found bugs planted in his house.

Not until Dashiell Bain, CIA spook, came into the room and shut the speakers off and sat down across from him.

Dash started with, "I know what you two had. Nate filled

me in."

"I know you slept with him," Rex countered.

"Did he tell you that?"

"No one had to tell me. I saw the way he looked at you."

Dash's jaw ticked. "I'll back off."

"Do you want to back off?"

"No," Dash said hoarsely, like it pained him to say so. "But I won't get in the way of a relationship."

That wasn't what Rex expected at all. "You're not sleeping with him for the job?"

"Started that way. I pretended it did. But now…"

"Did he say he wanted one with me?" Rex asked.

"No."

"Figured. He doesn't remember me or the relationship."

"How do you feel about him?"

"I'm always going to love him, Dash. But I'm in love with someone else. I'm really happy. I don't want to change that. Besides, I think Josh—Lucky—is falling for you."

Dash looked hopeful.

"Why are you really here, Dash?"

"Because I'm worried. Those bugs they found…they're ones that terrorist group used. The ones that captured you. The ones that captured me."

Rex stared at Dash. "Nate told me that."

"I figured he would."

"We're in the same goddamned place, Dash."

Dash's voice was raw when he said, "No, we're not. You

lost a hell of a lot more than I did."

"You were in captivity too," Rex said, and it looked like that statement hit Dash like a punch to the gut.

"You knew that the men who hurt us were never caught," Dash finally said.

"We weren't privy to that intel. I knew we wouldn't be sent back to get them but I was hoping, after all this time, that someone caught up to those bastards." Rex paused. "You're protecting your family. I can't blame you for investigating Lucky the way you've been—for tailing all of us. But who's protecting mine?"

"I will," Dash said.

11

"Sorry to keep you waiting. Is everything okay?"

Lucky glanced around the room where he'd been waiting for the past half an hour with his constant guard behind him and finally found the source of the voice.

A tall, dark-haired man in BDUs, who was holding the door open for the MP.

"It's fine," Lucky managed, and the man nodded and turned his attention to the MP, saying, "I've got this. Really. You can't be in here. Check with your CO—he'll tell you the same thing."

The MP finally conceded and the man who would be his psychiatrist from here on out closed the door and looked at him. "Better not to be guarded,right?"

"Much."

Since he'd been here, in this hospital, he'd spent most of his time locked in a private room on the psych floor. Before that, it was the brig for several days, until his tests came back and Dr. Larkin mentioned the possibility of some damage to his brain that could explain the memory loss.

Now that there was physical proof, he'd been released here. Granted, it was still a jail where they'd continue to assess him, see if he really had amnesia. Once they believed he wasn't a flight risk, he might be released but would still be required to attend these sessions and do everything he could in order to gain his memory back.

"I'm Dr. Randall Cooper. You can call me Cooper or Coop. Or Doc. Sometimes I'm sure you'll call me an asshole and it will hurt my feelings. But I'll live." His eyes were dark and like most of the other doctors around here, he was friendly. But he also seemed capable, in the way Rex, Nate and Uncle were.

In the way Dash had been.

It had been three weeks and Lucky hadn't seen any of them. To be fair, he hadn't asked but figured that the Navy was keeping him isolated for a reason.

He felt constantly watched.

Because you are.

Cooper was the one watching him now. "Josh, do you know why you're here?"

Here we go. No reason to hold back. "I don't know who the fuck Josh is. I've got amnesia but the Navy isn't convinced—everyone I've met isn't sure if I'm lying about that."

"Are you lying?"

"Look, I don't remember anything until four years ago when I swam to shore on a beach in South Africa. That's where my life begins. I'm not Josh—I'm Lucky."

"I can call you Lucky, if that helps."

"It helps because that's who I am."

Cooper nodded. Jotted something down. "This is fucking crazy," Lucky muttered.

"Why didn't you tell anyone you didn't have a memory when you first got to South Africa?"

He shrugged.

"Your first instinct was to lie."

"Yes."

"Why?"

"I don't know."

Cooper sat back. "I think you do. Was a part of you thinking like an operator?

Worried that people were after you? Were you doing it for self-protection?"

He probably had been.

"Holding it together in the face of that kind of memory loss, convincing people that you were okay, dealing with that takes a special kind of training. Did that ever occur to you?"

"At points, yes."

Cooper made a note in the file. "What else occurred to you?"

"Whenever anything did, I shoved it to the back of my mind," he admitted.

"Give me an example."

"I'm pretty strong."

"So are a lot of people."

"It's different for me. Once I realized it, I didn't get into fights. Didn't want to hurt anyone. But I kept wondering, if I was so strong, how did I get so hurt?"

"And how did you justify that? Maybe you weren't all that hurt," Cooper said, sounding slightly disinterested. Or maybe it was because he was writing instead of looking at Lucky and that pissed him off, more than he'd been since he arrived.

He'd been calm and stoic, because he'd known that was the way to stay out of trouble. But he was tired—of being prodded and poked physically, and now, they were going to fuck with his mind and tell him that he hadn't been hurt?

He stood and started to strip—shirt first, then he was undoing his hospital-issue scrubs and pulling them down and off. Cooper looked like he was about to tell him to stop, but Lucky wasn't stopping now. Cooper had asked for it.

When he was naked, he turned to show Cooper the scars. He heard the sharp intake of breath and he said, "Real thing's different than pictures, right, Doc?"

He stood there, letting Cooper see the torture he'd endured, a beating he didn't know the hows or whys about, a beating he deserved to know about. And he told Cooper that. Told him that he had no fucking clue what happened to him, but he wanted to.

"I need to," he told Cooper now. "And I'll work with you,

but you need to give me some goddamned answers, not more questions."

"I'm sorry, Lucky."

Lucky pulled his clothes on and prepared to leave. But he didn't. Instead, he sat across from a shaken Cooper, who said, "You have to let me help you. For your sake, not the Navy's. Yours."

For the first time since this started, Lucky said, "Okay," and meant it.

"I'm betting that most people, the Navy included, think it's easier that you don't remember?"

"Makes it worse, actually. But I can see their point—if you don't remember how bad things were, you won't have the trauma. But I know there was trauma. I don't know anything else. I didn't even know I was in the goddamned Navy."

"First thing you remember—quick, just let it all spill out."

More questions, but at least Lucky could see the purpose to these. Cooper wasn't going to find his feelings written in the pages of his medical test results.

"I remember the pain. The fear. It was freezing and I was underwater and I knew what to do. I didn't panic. How the hell does that happen? I was dumped in the middle of the ocean, tied, and I didn't panic. I got free and I started to rise to the surface. How would I even know which way that was? My head was killing me—my whole body hurt, but all that mattered was rising to the surface. And then, I kept feeling that panic of never being able to rise to the surface, never being able to grab at the memories. So I just tried to get on with my life and I was scared and in pain, but after that initial panic, it didn't happen again. Not even when the Navy came to getme."

"Were you angry about that?" He shrugged.

"Not at the Navy."

"At who, then?"

Dash, mainly. But he shook his head. "I don't want to do this."

He was up out of his seat, until Cooper said, "If you run, you don't have to deal with any of it, right?"

"Right. I know that. I have amnesia, not idiocy." Cooper stared at him.

"What do you want me to say? I'm happy?"

"I want you to tell me the truth, whatever it is. I can deal with it, no matter how ugly you think it is or how stupid you think it might sound."

"I'm gay." Cooper nodded.

"I mean, Josh was gay. And I'm gay."

"So you're giving me the born-this-way argument."

"I guess so. I mean, if I was trying to lie, wouldn't I pretend to be straight?"

"I don't know. Would you?"

"You're doing it again."

Cooper smiled. "Force of habit. Does being gay bother

you?"

"No. Not remembering the man I had a long relationship with does. Not remembering how old I am, when my birthday was, where my family is bothers the hell out of me. And I'm betting you've been told to keep that shit from me until you can assess me further."

"You're right."

"Then what do we talk about?"

"Why don't you tell me about South Africa?"

That was, for the most part, a good memory, and he smiled involuntarily.

"Anything that makes you smile like that is definitely worth talking about, so yes, let's talk about that," Cooper murmured.

For the next several hours, Lucky did.

12

Cooper went to his desk, flipped through the papers for a few minutes. He was muttering to himself—Dash caught something about all the goddamned paperwork and the goddamned caseload and then he grabbed a coffee cup and drank it down. Grimaced.

Dash had been there. Sometimes, you needed caffeine more than taste buds. "Do you think he's lying?" he asked now.

Cooper nearly choked, put a hand over his heart and the cup down. He turned to see Dash sitting on the desk.

"Trying to kill me?"

"If I was…"

"Yeah, yeah, I'd already be dead. Got it." Cooper picked at the edge of Lucky's file. "I figured they'd send you."

"I figured they'd just tell you."

"That too. The fact that this is all confidential doesn't matter to you?"

"Not to the CIA. And that's who you chose to work for."

"Lucky thinks I work for the Navy."

"I'm betting he's smart enough to realize that nothing around here is anything close to what it seems."

Cooper rubbed his chin. "Didn't realize the CIA could break the goddamned patient confidentiality rules."

"Even if the man being investigated might be a risk to national security?"

Cooper sighed. "Either he's got amnesia or he's the best liar I've ever met. And I've met a lot of them. And none of you can fool me."

"None of us?"

"You all have a tell."

"What's mine?"

"I'm not sharing that with you. But you do have one. And the reason you're here has less to do with the job and more to do with your feelings for Lucky."

"That's a guess."

"I don't guess," Cooper told him. "I don't think he's lying. I believe he's got zero memory before four years ago. And I'm not sure if bringing his memory back is in anyone's best interest."

Dash nodded. "Keep trying anyway. No one's interested in your personal opinions."

"Fuck you, Dash."

"Cooper…"

"If you think he's just a job, you're lying to yourself."

Yes, he was, but the last person he'd admit it to was the company shrink. "Do you think he'll get his memory back?"

"We've been trying a lot of techniques and he's been open to them. But if sodium pentothal isn't working—"

"Hypnosis?"

"He can't be hypnotized."

"Because he was trained not to be?"

"Maybe. Who can say? There are civilians who can't be hypnotized."

"I saw his brain scans."

"There's damage. Mild, but it's near the memory bank. It makes sense that nothing else is really affected except his pain sensors."

"What's that about?" Dash asked.

"He feels pain more easily because his body's always on alert—damaged nerve endings. Hard to tell if that's from the brain injury or the beatings he endured."

Dash couldn't help but wince.

"I saw the scars. He stripped for me."

Dash felt the lunge of jealousy, and he took a step toward Cooper before he could stop himself. Cooper merely grinned.

"Don't hurt him, Coop."

"Not in the job description, Dash. Unless he's got plans to hurt his country."

"So if he's not getting his memory back, can he leave?"

"Soon, yes."

"Got to be more to the story."

"We're not letting him out of the Navy yet. He can stay in

town, meet with me, and the Navy will subsidize him with disability. Has to check in with me weekly."

"What's he supposed to do?"

Cooper shrugged. "He's got full access to the gym."

"Jesus."

"I'm planning on releasing him to an apartment right off base next week. There's no reason for us to keep him when his brain scan shows damage that supports his memory loss. He hasn't slipped up a single time in two months—and trust me, we've done everything we could beyond recreating the torture. Plus, we've interrogated his SEAL teammates. There's nothing suspicious. Nothing even remotely so."

"Except that he was dumped near my family, Cooper," he growled, and Cooper tilted his head in acknowledgement. "How can I ever trust that he wasn't put there to hurt them?"

"I'm not saying the terrorist who captured Lucky didn't try to turn him. We don't know what happened between the boat and the beach, and we might never know."

The terrorist was named Allen Gonzalves—they didn't say his name out loud. Dash had buried it deeply, or else he would've turned into a machine bent solely on revenge.

Allen Gonzalves and his army ruined men's lives. And he was still out there.

"You still haven't told him why he's really here," Dash said. "He thinks it's because he's highly trained. He's worried he might have a temper, might kill someone accidentally. When are you going to tell him he's suspected of being a traitor?"

"He knows that much."

"But he doesn't know everything. You need to tell him that and see what happens."

"I have a plan, Dashiell. He's been hinting about talking to Rex. I'm going to let him when he comes right out and asks."

It wasn't a bad idea—hearing it come from Rex could trigger memories. But hell, that would be one painful session. "And after that? Suppose it doesn'twork?"

"Then we're done."

"That's it? You won't keep trying to get Lucky's memories back?" Dash asked.

"If it doesn't trigger anything, we're going to keep trying to get the memories back. But I think if he's got some freedom, maybe we'll find out more."

"Loosen the leash," Dash said.

"Yes. And I've got some other plans for him. But I wanted him to have someone with him who he feels might be on his side."

"And that's me?"

"I'm guessing you're going to be his personal bodyguard?" Cooper asked.

"Why would you say that?"

"That's what your supervisor told me when he called."

"You're still an asshole, Coop, you know that?"

"Have to be to keep up with all of you."

"I want to talk with my old teammates. Can I do that?" Lucky asked Cooper. After three more weeks of various psych tests, including and not limited to sodium pentothal, hypnosis and lie detector tests, all of which yielded zero results and more frustration for him, he was ready to see if hearing about an actual memory of his might trigger an avalanche.

"I can arrange that."

"But I'll have to do it on tape, right?"

"Not if they come in here."

"You'd do that?"

"Yes, I would. I agree that it might help and it definitely won't hurt. And I can understand you having reservations about sharing things with outsiders, because you don't know what you might not be able to say. Like, about your relationship with Rex."

"I know Don't Ask Don't Tell's been repealed, but..."

"But you were on the same team and that might be frowned upon. Granted, neither of you were officers, so you can't be accused of fraternizing, and you were the same rank," Cooper said. Lucky took all that information and filed it away in his brain.

He was going to need to start keeping a binder of all the people, places and things Josh had in his life.

Now, twenty-four hours later, Lucky sat with Rex on the couch. Nate and Uncle would come in for the next session, but since Rex knew the most about him, Cooper said this would be better as a one on one.

A one on one with Cooper sitting behind his desk trying to give them as much privacy as possible.

"Thanks for doing this," Lucky said, staring at the big man with the shaved head and the intense gaze.

"We've been trying to see you—me and Nate and Uncle."

Lucky felt his throat tighten that these men, who knew they were total strangers to him, would be waiting there to help him.

"Cooper told me that you haven't been able to remember anything. He said I can answer your questions, but I can't offer any information you don't ask about. And if anything I say triggers your memories…"

"You'll be the first to know."

"Smartass," Rex muttered. "Was I always?"

"Uh, yeah."

Lucky slid his hands together, glad they'd started out on that note. Rex opened one of the sodas on the table in front of them and handed it to Lucky. Lucky took a sip as

Rex opened one of his own, telling Lucky, "Your life wasn't anything to be scared about."

"Okay, yeah. What about my family? Are they freaking out about this? Have they even been told?"

Rex took a long drink from his soda. "I was your family, Lucky. Still am."

"I'm an orphan?"

"Yes. You came up through the foster-care system—you were abandoned as an infant."

"Where?"

Rex shifted. "You were left in a box in the hallway of an apartment building. They estimated you were maybe an hour old. No one ever came forward to claim you."

"And I wasn't adopted?"

"Almost. But you were pulled from a few placements. You never knew why. Maybe it was abuse. Who knows. But you went into group homes."

"And then I went into the Navy."

"You enlisted at seventeen when you got kicked out of the system and a judge signed off on your papers. You enlisted in the Navy because you wanted to fly helos. And you were on that track until you showed other proficiencies. And that's when they put you into BUD/s and no matter how bad it got—and it got bad—you refused to quit." Rex tilted his head. "You didn't ask me what BUD/s was."

Lucky smiled. "I do have access to a computer. And the Navy's website." He slid a glance toward Cooper who said,

"You're not supposed to have access."

Rex snickered.

"Okay, so why didn't I quit? Couldn't I have gone back to flying choppers then?"

"Probably. They always say there's no shame in ringing out. They'd rather you know your limits before you put a teammate at risk."

"I don't get it. I put myself through Hell Week so I could go through more hell—"

"I found you researched Hell Week on my computer's history," Cooper interjected. "—on every single mission," Lucky finished. "Why?"

"You told me it was because you didn't know any other way," Rex told him quietly.

"What the hell did I go through in foster care?" Lucky asked. "Or is this something else you're going to tell me it's better I don't remember?"

Rex sighed. Rubbed his shaved head.

"Forget it."

"I don't want to be the one who has to tell you all the bad shit. That's how you're going to know me."

"I thought you think of me as family?" Lucky asked. "Don't they always say no one hurts you more, knows you better than family? Because I'd rather hear this shit from you than from some random shrink. Unless I'm not considered your family anymore."

"I will always consider you family," Rex said, his voice

raw. "Don't doubt that." Lucky nodded.

"You were pretty knocked around as a kid. You had a special knack for finding trouble. And I think that's why you ended up being so good at evading the truth, because it stopped you from getting into trouble. And then you got big, so they stopped hitting you. But you were too big and a lot of the families didn't want you, even though you were gentle. So you stayed in group homes and you found ways to keep yourself occupied."

"Is that a nice way of saying I broke the law?"

Rex snorted. "Yes."

"What do I know how to do?"

"You can hotwire cars faster than anyone I've met. You were good at anything mechanical. You could rebuild engines and make them purr. I'm betting that if I put you in a garage, you'd know exactly what to do."

"If they ever let me out of here, I'll take you up on it." He paused. "Are we going to be in trouble because we were together?"

"Coop's not going to say anything to the top brass. This is more to help you," Rex said.

Lucky looked at Cooper, who still had his head down, taking notes.

"And I won't hold the random shrink comment against you," Cooper said, without looking up.

"So we met in BUD/s. I'm guessing we got close. But is that when we got together?" Rex nodded. "We had a friendship. It all happened fast and furious. HellWeek doesthat,forms strong bonds. And after that, it was work and sex, and everything melded together."

Lucky stared at the big man, tried to imagine being in his arms. Rex was attractive as hell and maybe if Dash wasn't constantly in the forefront of his mind he wouldn't have to imagine an attraction. It would simply be there. But right now…nothing. "Did we fight?"

"Yes."

"Over what?"

"Control."

"Obviously not in the bedroom."

Rex snorted. "We didn't have issues there."

"And you're with someone else now."

"Yeah. His name's Sawyer. He's a SEAL."

"Guess you have a type," Lucky said before he could stop himself and heard Cooper choke on his coffee. Rex was at least smiling. "So things are good?"

"I think so. It's still all new. Took a long time for him to admit his feelings for me."

"Scared because you're his CO?"

"Scared because he didn't think he was gay." Lucky raised a brow. "He's bi."

"Can't help who you fall in love with," Lucky said quietly.

"Who did you fall for?" Rex asked now but Lucky shook his head. Still, he had a feeling Rex knew. The way he'd watched Dash walk away at the airport in South Africa, he figured it was obvious to a blind man.

"I guess it's enough to know I haven't forgotten how, right?" He leaned back against the couch. He'd been so tense, like he'd been bracing for a flood of memories. Now that nothing was happening, he realized how much he needed to know about his life. "How old am I?"

"Thirty-six," Rex told him. "A year older than me. Your birthday's November sixth."

"I told her my birthday was in April, but Emme always insisted I was a Scorpio." Rex smiled, like maybe they'd had this conversation before about astrological signs.

Lucky glanced toward Cooper. The shrink had said he'd rather Lucky find out about his capture here, in the hospital, in case he had a bad reaction. "Why's the CIA involved?"

"You might not remember being a SEAL, but you definitely have an operator's instincts," Rex told him. "For the mission we were captured on, the CIA sanctioned us to retire a terrorist who kidnapped two CIA agents and beheaded one of them on national TV."

"And the other agent?"

Rex shifted. Glanced at Cooper then back at Lucky.

"Rex, they're acting like I can take down the free world."

"Because they're worried you were turned. That this is all an act."

"Turned?"

"By the terrorists who captured us."

A chill went through Lucky, and as he went still, so did

Rex and Cooper. "I…I didn't see that coming. Jesus, they think I'm a terrorist? That I've been hiding for four years. Working as a bartender?"

"South African shoreline…a good spot to sneak terrorists into Africa without notice. You could be a conduit. Or you could have other plans. Terrorists are a notoriously patient bunch."

"I didn't even remember 9/11. Emme was watching a special on it. I recognized it from some of Dash's pictures. I pretended but I stayed up all night researching it. I was already in the Navy when it happened, according to Cooper."

Rex nodded. "Our team went right into action after that. Hunted down a lot of them, took them out. You helped a lot."

"And now they think I've defected." He paused. "They're never going to be satisfied. They'll haunt me forever, just in case something pops up."

"They won't let you leave the country. Maybe not the state without an escort until they're satisfied you're not working with the terrorists."

Which was never going to happen unless he could prove, beyond a shadow of a doubt, that his memories would never return, or that he'd never been in collusion with the enemy.

He rubbed his forehead like he could bring the memories out, but they weren't even skirting his consciousness.

"Our team went in to save the CIA agents and we were captured." He didn't want to go further into the actual methods of capture and torture, not then. Maybe it was more because he didn't want Rex to have to relive it. But they were coming perilously close to having no choice but to deal with it.

"Right."

"What did you think happened to me?"

Rex's face clouded. Lucky didn't want to go there any more than Rex did. But if they wanted memories from him, he'd have to try to trigger them any way he could.

Cooper said Lucky would probably need something harsh to break the amnesia. That it might happen now or ten years from now.

Or never.

"We were put into separate cells. Beaten on a rotating basis. Given a day to heal, listen to the rest of us getting hit. We were each told we could make it stop. Standard shit."

"But they did let you go, right?"

Rex blinked. Stared. "We were let go about two days after they told us you died."

A chill went through Lucky as Rex talked about his death. He didn't remember any of this—it was like being told the plot to a movie. And Lucky wanted all the spoilers, but it was strange being so detached and so invested in the outcome all at the same time. "Did you think the terrorists killed me?"

"No. It was an infection in your leg. They wouldn't give you medical treatment, no matter how hard we begged. They'd only do it if we did what they wanted us to. And we couldn't. You have to understand that we couldn't."

"I do, Rex. You couldn't give in."

"Fuck." Rex rubbed his head and the pain in his eyes was unmistakable. "If they'd wanted something else, I would've given it to them. If they'd said to me, 'Your life for his', I would've let them kill me."

"Don't say that."

"It's the truth, Lucky. It's what you need to hear. I would've saved your life if that was all it would've taken."

That weighed heavily on Lucky, and he wondered how much someone could take on before he broke.

Rex continued, "They showed us your body. They threw you into a fire, said they didn't want infection to spread, which was bullshit. I figured they just didn't want us to be able to bring your body home."

Lucky nodded. Everything was bits and pieces of a puzzle that wasn't fitting together quite right for him.

"So why wouldn't they have done the same thing with me that they did with that agent? Why not show my body to the world on videotape?"

Lucky didn't realize he was indicting Rex with that statement, realized it only after the anger in Rex's voice came out. "At the time, we didn't know what they'd done to that agent. We were being held, remember."

"I didn't mean it like that, Rex. I have twenty-twenty hindsight," he started, but Rex cut him off.

"Let me see your leg. Your calf." Rex's voice sounded hoarse and then he was kneeling at Lucky's feet.

Lucky felt like he should pull away, that Rex wasn't going to like what he found. But he didn't, let Rex pull up the scrub pants, which were all Lucky was allowed to wear in here.

And then Rex held his bared calf in both hands and stared at it like something was really wrong. Ran his hands around the back, lifted it like it wasn't attached to Lucky.

"I don't understand this," he muttered. He went for the other calf, did the same thing. "Nothing. Not fucking possible."

"Want to tell me what you're looking for?" Lucky asked.

Rex sat back on his heels, his eyes dark, an obvious temper rising. He looked angry and confused, and Lucky steeled himself. Fought for a scrap of memory and found none. He stared down at his calves, wondering what Rex had expected to find. "Do your scars go all the way down to your calves?"

The question seemed to wake Rex up. "No."

"Mine stop at the back of my knees."

"Mine too," Rex said.

"Then what are you looking for?"

"Nothing. Guess I got confused."

"And now you're lying."

Rex glanced up at him, seemed to remember he was on the floor and pushed himself to his feet. Lucky fixed his pants, trying not to let the panic rise.

Rex started slowly. "They told us that you had an infection in your leg. That you had a fever. They said it was killing you and under those conditions…"

Rex had already told him this, so Lucky was even more confused. "Did you see the infection?"

"No. There was a bandage on your leg. And you were so out of it. Glassy eyes. Lethargic. None of us were in great condition but you looked like…" He paused before he uttered the word *death*.

Lucky stared. "Guess it wasn't me."

"The men who held us, they showed us a picture of your leg infection. It was down to the bone in your leg—and then they told us that they'd get you medical attention if we turned. When we didn't…fuck, that's when they burned a body that was supposedly yours. Christ, we were all so out of it, drugged and beaten, and you'd been so out of it the last time they dragged you past the room I was being tortured in. But now, this doesn't make sense. There should be a goddamned scar. Maybe I got the leg wrong, but there should be a scar."

"But there's not. So what does that mean?"

Cooper had intervened not long after Rex went looking for the scar on Lucky's legs and found none. Rex had looked angry and apologetic when he left, escorted out by Cooper.

Lucky could just imagine the conversation the two of them were having.

In the meantime, he pulled up his own pants to stare down at his calves. Other than some small scars here and there, there was zero indication that he'd had a severe, life-threatening infection.

Cooper came back into the room then, shut the door behind him, and Lucky was so drained. He hoped that Cooper wasn't going to keep him here for much longer. His head spun, his fucking heart hurt.

"Tell me what you're thinking," Cooper said quietly, although it was more of a demand than Lucky had ever heard from the man.

"I don't have the scars on my leg."

"So? Rex himself said he was being beaten daily. Starved. Maybe drugged."

Lucky nodded. It would be so easy to believe what Cooper was telling him, what Rex told him earlier. God, he wanted to, so damned badly. But… "What if…what if I did agree to help them in exchange for my team's life and then…" He shook his head. "Why go to all that trouble and then beat the shit out of me and dump me in the ocean? That doesn't make sense."

"What does makes sense to you about it?"

He glanced at Cooper. "I'm not playing the speculation game with you."

"Why not? Afraid of what you might find?"

"Look, I don't remember shit. And now, a member of my team is actually starting to doubt my story. So fuck this."

He stood, stormed out of the office, not turning back when Cooper called his name.

At this point, he was still a prisoner. And he wasn't going back to therapy unless they locked him in and forced him. Which they probably would, come morning.

He circled back to his room, going through the locked ward doors with the soldier- slash-guard silently following him. The guy must have orders to not talk to him ever, so it was like having a ghost trailing him. He wondered when— if—the guy ever slept. Or if he was a twin. Or if everyone and everything was starting to look alike to him, because maybe if you spent enough time in a mental ward, you became mental.

He wondered if Dash would come in for a session. That would be worth going back to Cooper and asking. And then he could finally process the truth behind the fact that Dash had used him to get intel. That he was a job to Dash.

No matter how much he told himself it hadn't felt like that, even when Dash handed him over to his old SEAL team, Lucky knew he had to come to terms with the truth.

No one's ever going to fully trust you. And how the hell was he supposed to live with that?

14

Sawyer hadn't seen Rex for six weeks, since the night he'd come home for the party. After that, Sawyer and the team, with their XO stepping in for Rex, had gone on a month- long mission. When they'd returned home, Sawyer slept on base to finish his SITREP.

He knew Rex was still going through hell, being called in for debriefings about the capture. He wondered if Rex's career was in jeopardy, but more than that, he was worried about Rex.

At first, Rex checked in by text. Sawyer wanted to hear his voice but knew that would upset both of them further. Although he wasn't really sure Rex was upset at all, at least not about the fact that he wasn't spending time with Sawyer.

"I know he's being watched, but I also know he's totally fucking avoiding me," he told Jace now as he finished lunch at Jace's house.

"Didn't sound like he avoided you the night of the party."

"That was sex."

Jace nodded. "Sex is always easier than anything else.

But you would've been more worried if he didn't fuck you, am I right?"

"You just like hearing you're right," Sawyer mumbled, hating to admit that Jace had a point. "He wouldn't talk much about it. Said he couldn't."

"Well, that's partially true. But I'm guessing he figures it's weird for you." Sawyer shrugged. "Weirder pretending it's not happening."

"Did you tell him that, or are you going to share shit he can't possibly know now with me only?" Jace asked.

Sawyer threw a fork at him, and Jace ducked. The fork rattled in the wall, tongs embedded.

"Next time, I won't miss on purpose."

"Keep telling yourself that."

Sawyer drove back to base, Jace on his Harley behind Sawyer's truck. They were early for the meeting, fucked around for a few minutes with their other team members, and Sawyer was grateful none of them mentioned the Josh situation.

Rex looked fucking wrecked when he'd walked into the meeting room that morning. Sawyer sat on his hands, forced to pretend it was all business as usual, had to watch the man he'd fallen in love with go over a SITREP with the team and then delve into their upcoming mission plans.

To Rex's credit, he looked like hell but he didn't miss a beat. By this time, the entire team knew about Josh, so they all sat quietly and respectfully, with none of the usual banter that went along with mission planning.

And then, when the meeting ended, it was time for training. Sawyer was surprised that Rex was leading the exercises, but he took it as a good sign. Maybe things with Lucky were looking up.

And Rex was doing his usual yelling, the way he always did before a mission. Except this time, he stepped it up a notch, and Sawyer got it. They'd spent time apart and Rex was freaked and he'd push Sawyer and the rest of the team to hell and back, just to make sure they never actually got that far.

But pushing and riding were two different things, and Sawyer was precariously close to breaking. Jace knew it, tried to deflect some of Rex's yelling while still keeping Sawyer on track. And Rex seemed to have no problem yelling at Jace either, and more than usual.

Sawyer held out for four hours. And then he couldn't stand it anymore. Maybe if Rex had called or texted or did anything since fucking and running...

"You can't let it affect you."

Jace was right. But Sawyer had gone from getting an amazing write-up from the admiral to this, being yelled at in front of the two new guys and anyone in their general vicinity because he hadn't been able to shave time from the O-course runs.

"What've you been doing since I've been gone? Sitting on your ass?" It was a blanket statement to all of them, but he got right in Sawyer's face when he yelled it. It took everything Sawyer had not to give him a satisfying head-butt and Rex knew it, told him, "What're you going to do? Take me down? Go ahead and try it."

Instead, Sawyer did the course again, shaved the time and then did it twice more just to prove he could. When he finished, Rex was gone and Jace was telling him that he was staying with him and Clint until he calmed the fuck down.

Sawyer didn't argue, because being alone right now wouldn't have helped anything. And he let Jace do all the bitching on the car ride back to Jace's. Jace loaded his bike into the back of Sawyer's truck to make things easier.

"Because there's no way I can keep my goddamned balance after that shit," Jace grumbled. "I know he's always like that to you, but how the hell did I get on Rex's good side?"

"Clint."

"Clint talked to him?"

"He called one night."

"And you're just telling me this now?"

"My misery likes your company."

"Yeah, I'll bet."

Sawyer parked, still in an angry daze. He found himself sitting at Jace's table, staring at nothing in particular, pushing away Jace's offers of food.

He wanted to talk about it, but really, what the hell was he supposed to say?

"Hey bud." Clint's voice. He sat down next to Sawyer, a look of sympathy on his face.

"Guess the whole goddamned world knows."

"Yeah, pretty much. POWs are a big deal."

"Shit. I know. Hell, I'm glad he's alive, glad they found him. It's just…it changes everything."

"Doesn't have to," Clint said.

"It already has." Just then, Sawyer's phone rang. Rex. He pressed the speaker button and Rex said, "Come to my house, now."

"You can go fuck yourself, *sir.* I'll see you on base."

Clint raised his brows, and he and Jace left the room so Sawyer could talk in privacy.

"You'll come here and see me now," Rex said again, calmly.

"Don't do this, Rex. I won't."

"I will spank the shit out of you," Rex warned him, his voice low.

"Yeah, you try that and you'll find yourself through the goddamned wall."

Sawyer could handle a lot of things, but spanking wasn't one of them. He'd learned that early on with Rex, when even the threat of it made him angry instead of turned on.

"I wasn't going to do it for pleasure, Sawyer. You don't think I know you well enough?"

Rex did, and that's what made this harder. "Try your Dom punishment shit on someone else."

"I don't want to try it on anyone but you."

"I'm not willing. Isn't that what you always said—that it had to be safe, sane and consensual?"

"Keep pushing, boy."

Boy always did it to Sawyer, made the blood rush to his cock faster than anything. He didn't know why that did it for him, but Rex knew that it did and used it to exploit his weakness.

"Want to let it out?" Rex asked.

"What?"

"You going for sainthood?"

"Fuck you, Rex. Handling this the best way I can."

"You're too fucking understanding. And you're pulling away. Distancing yourself from me. You started the night before I left for South Africa."

"Because I can see the writing on the wall. Because I don't want to deal. Because…"

"It's the thing that's always bothered you," Rex said softly.

"Don't patronize me."

"You want out?"

Sawyer stared at the table in front of him. He'd been biting back anger and tears for the past couple of weeks and he didn't think he could anymore.

"Do you want out? Things get a little tough and you want out?"

"Is that what you want me to want?"

"I wanted you to stop acting like a goddamned saint. I

know things are bothering you."

"And pushing me was the way to force me to say it?"

"Only thing that seemed to work." Rex paused. "I need you to help me."

"I'm letting you use me as a punching bag. What more do you want?"

"Come to my house. Pull in the garage and wait for me."

He was about to protest when Rex said, "You're going to get what you need. But only if you shut your mouth and get here now."

Rex hung up and Sawyer stared at the phone stupidly.

"Go to him," Clint said.

"Why?"

"Dom voice," Jace said with a smile, and Clint put a hand on the back of Jace's neck. "It's a good sign."

Rex hadn't used it in a while. Not since they were together a lot of the time.

They'd been together, but not *together*. And before he could ruminate on how stupid that sounded, he said goodnight to Jace and Clint and he was in his car, driving to see Rex. His heart was beating fast, fingers drumming the wheel, not knowing what lay beyond the garage doors.

But he pulled into the opened side and he waited. The door came down behind the car and he cracked his door and started to getout.

"Can't follow simple directions?"

Rex's voice. Sawyer stilled, not wanting to get yelled at

again. But Rex's voice was different, almost playful, and Sawyer wanted to hate him.

In reality, he probably did. He pulled back into the car and shut the door and stared straight ahead.

After what seemed like hours, Rex opened his door and said, "Come with me."

"Rex…I don't need you to pretend."

Rex's expression softened for a second. "I've never had to pretend with you. I don't intend to start now."

Sawyer followed him, out of the car, into the house and into the bedroom.

"Strip." Rex told him.

"Rex—"

"Didn't ask for talking. Clothes off. Or leave."

Sawyer looked at the floor and wondered why the hell he was putting up with this shit. Until Rex put a hand on the back of his neck and said, "Please."

He drew in a breath and he stripped. Looked at Rex and the heat in the man's eyes, and things became clearer. He'd known why Rex was ultra-freaked, but knowing and dealing with it were two different things.

This was Rex's apology. And, like the man said, all Sawyer needed to do was accept it.

"Still thinking," Rex grunted. "Get on the bed. On your belly."

Sawyer complied, feeling strangely vulnerable and completely, undeniably turned on at the same time. Rex took his time winding the soft ropes around Sawyer's wrists, tight enough to hold him in place but still comfortable enough that his circulation wouldn't be compromised.

"I'm keeping you here like this for a while. Until you stop thinking. Until you calm the fuck down. And I'm going to help you, babe. Trust me," Rex told him.

Sawyer nodded, then turned his cheek to the pillow and watched Rex surveying him, spread-eagled, unable, and at this point very willing to remain unable, to move.

"You could escape if you really wanted to. I know that. But you won't, because you like the way you feel. Don't you?"

"Yes." God, he did. His body finally relaxed and his mind actually followed. It happened during sex, but this was a whole other thing. And Rex's voice was making him calmer and hornier, all at once.

He'd refused spankings. He liked the commands in theory and on the phone, but when they were together, he just wanted Rex. But Rex wanted to give him something more—needed to—and Sawyer obviously needed it just as much.

Rex ran a hand along Sawyer's back, and he shuddered under the contact. "Did you like what we Skyped about last month?"

"Yes."

"This is exactly how I pictured you, tied in your bunk. Naked. Spread. And your bunkmates could come back in at any second and find you."

"Rex…"

Rex's hands separated his ass, and Sawyer felt him blow warm breath. His hole twitched, and he buried his head into the pillow as embarrassment fought the fantasy.

"You're blushing. But you want it, don't you, baby?"

Sawyer's "Yes" came out muffled. Rex grabbed him by the hair and lifted his head up.

"I want to hear it louder."

"Yes."

"More detailed."

"Fuck."

"That's for me to decide. Answer my question."

"Yes, Rex, I want it, want you eating my ass."

"Then you better beg for it. Because we don't have much time before we're caught."

Just like that, Rex brought him into the fantasy. Completely. He was in the bunk, in the dark, and instead of jacking off quietly, Rex had buried his face in his ass.

He bit the pillow to keep back the groans, the way he'd have to if they were really in the bunk. Rex didn't let up on him, and Sawyer was tied tightly enough that it was hard for him to buck against the bed to give himself relief.

"Please," he whimpered.

"I think I hear them coming back. You'd better make it quick. Although, I'm going to need you to come twice before I even consider letting you up."

Sawyer buried his face into the pillow as Rex spread his ass and buried his face, tonguing him with hard strokes, alternating with spearing his tongue to enter him. He jerked hard against the mattress, unable to stop himself from coming immediately, but Rex didn't stop. Not when Sawyer yanked against the ropes, not when he begged, because even he didn't know what he was begging for.

The second orgasm surprised him as much as the first.

"You want me to fuck you, boy?"

"Please…"

"The only way I'm going to let you up is if you tell me that's what you want. Or maybe you'd rather me invite the others in here to watch."

Holy good shit. Rex entered him as he spoke, and Sawyer could almost feel the strangers crowding in around them, watching.

"Yeah, they'd come in and watch you getting the fucking of your life. Wondering if I'll let them take a turn next. Think I should?" he asked as he thrust several times in a row, fast and hard enough to make Sawyer's prostatesing.

"Please," was all Sawyer could manage, because he was there, but he wasn't. He was off someplace, his body a maze of pleasure, and he couldn't find his way to the root of it. But he didn't care.

The next orgasm was a dry one, but it didn't matter. He felt Rex coming inside him, then the man pulled out in order to finish spurting along Sawyer's back.

And then Sawyer was completely, one hundred and fifty percent satiated. Flying but somehow not needing to move at all. He was boneless. And he couldn't remember being happier.

Sawyer was vaguely aware of Rex untying him. He might've passed out or fallen asleep or any combination of the two, and Rex didn't seem to mind. He massaged Sawyer's shoulders and arms and legs, getting rid of the pins and needles. He made Sawyer drink some soda. He cleaned him up.

And Sawyer, who'd normally be jumping out of bed, just lay there, enjoying the hell out of all of it.

When Rex finally lay down next to him, he threw a leg over Sawyer possessively.

"Thank you," he told Sawyer.

"Shouldn't I be the one thanking you?"

"You really don't know how much I get out of doing that? No, you don't. I forgot it myself for a really long time. I put that part of myself away with Josh and that was okay then. But I did miss it. And I realize how much I need it."

"Why did you put it away with Josh?"

"I didn't think we needed it. But that's not really the point. Sometimes it's not about needing as much as it is about want. And sometimes it's both."

Sawyer smiled, still feeling like he was floating. "Is it selfish of me to admit I like having a part of you that you didn't share with him?"

"I'd imagine I'd feel the same way." Rex stroked his hair. "You're still in sub-space."

"I like it here."

"I like bringing you here. Look how still you are."

He was—still and relaxed, and for the first time in months, years maybe, his mind was clear. "I think this needs to become a part of our repertoire."

"I certainly wouldn't mind it." Rex smiled. "This trust is the next step. I know you trust me with your life but do you trust me to take control of your emotions? Because that's a whole new level of trust."

"Did I pass the test?"

"I don't test you, baby. I make sure you love what I do to you. For you. And I think it's apparent that you loved this."

"I love you, Rex."

"I never get tired of hearing you say that." Rex looked so serious. "I fucking love you, Sawyer. Nothing's going to change that."

"I'm sorry that things with Josh—Lucky—have been so difficult."

Rex's expression darkened. "I think I really fucked up with him. I went into one of his therapy sessions and he was asking me questions. And I went to look for the scar on his leg, because the infection I saw was really bad. It would've left one. And there was nothing. No scars on his legs. And I'm guessing if I'm misremembering where the infection was, if there were scars on other parts of his body from an infection, he would've shown me."

"So what are you thinking? You don't think he agreed to help them in exchange for your lives?"

"Two days after he was killed, we were released."

"You weren't rescued?"

"No. That never made any goddamned sense to any of us."

"Okay, so the infection was a ruse," Sawyer said. "Why go to all that trouble? And why would you think there would be a scar?"

"There were pictures. The CIA found the ones we were shown in captivity. They had pictures of a deep infection. You could see bone."

Sawyer stared. "You're really beginning to suspect him."

"I don't want to. But we went through hell."

"And you told him that the Josh you knew never would've broken."

Rex hung his head. "What if I was wrong, Sawyer? What if…"

"He doesn't remember. I don't care how good a liar someone is. You can't fake that.

He would've slipped by now."

"I hope you're right." Rex sighed. "It's good that you brought Clint in when you were followed, because that led to finding the bugs. I'm glad you stayed with them."

"After that, there were no more followings, no more bugs planted."

"That doesn't mean the danger's not there." Rex shook his head. "I thought this was over, but it's so far from that. I might still be in danger. I might've put you in danger. I feel like shit that he was left behind. I keep thinking, were there any clues that he was still alive? Did they drug us to make us believe we saw his body being put into the fire? And even though I know there wasn't anything we could've done… seeing him not even remember his own age is tough."

"How is he, though?"

"He's better than I am about it. He's frustrated, sure. But I think… " Rex paused. "I think he's actually all right. And that's what's getting me through all of it. Because hell, if he doesn't have to have the nightmares, why would I wish that on him? Or on anyone."

Sawyer ran a hand down Rex's biceps, feeling the strong muscle. Tried to imagine how baditwas. He'd only been trapped fortwenty-four hours and that had felt like a lifetime. And no one had been beating him or Jace during that time.

"I'm not going to be able to stop pushing you on the field. You know that," Rex said.

Sawyer did. Rex didn't yell like that on missions. Once they were in it, they were a well-oiled machine. But before, Rex would do everything in his power to make sure noone made a mistake that would get them killed or captured. "What was the mistake?" he asked now and Rex furrowed his brow. "On that mission—what was the mistake?"

He waited for Rex to get angry, to walk out, and Sawyer wondered if he'd ruined whatever ground they'd made up tonight.

"We knew we might get captured and we went in anyway. We figured we had a better shot of getting in and out of there than anyone else. And we couldn't stand to think that they had agents incaptivity."

Rex drew a deep breath after he spoke, like it was maybe the first time he'd admitted it to anyone out loud.

"I don't consider that a mistake."

Rex glanced at him. "Hubris."

"Heroism."

"Don't try to make me feel better."

"If you had it to do all over again, you wouldn't change anything. That much I know."

"Fuck you," Rex said, but it was with a smile. "Knew there was a price for letting you in."

"If I can't get away with bullshitting myself, neither can you."

"I'm done with bullshitting myself. Lucky doesn't remember me. And I'm looking back and I'm wondering if we ever knew each other. And I don't want to make that mistake with you. I want you to know me. I'm tired of holding back. Josh's return has to mean something, and I want it to mean that I'm going to stop holding back."

And that meant Sawyer would have to stop doing so as well. As he made that silent deal with himself to do so, he felt Rex's hand snake around his waist to pull him even closer.

15

Lucky had been through almost three months of near solitary confinement, endless sessions with Cooper, meetings with top naval brass, including the admiral who'd been in charge of his SEAL team. Admiral Bobs looked visibly shaken after seeing Lucky, and he'd been kinder than Lucky had braced himself for.

And finally—finally—he was told he'd be allowed out of the facility. But he wasn't able to leave the general vicinity, and, after much discussion he hadn't been privy to, he'd been placed under surveillance in an apartment that was close to, but not on, base.

He knew why—they didn't want him anyplace he could do damage to a military facility—but he didn't care. He was free. One step closer to being out of this mess.

There were lawyers involved too, JAGs assigned to him. Both were sympathetic to his plight, and especially so after Cooper's evals came through.

There were no memories. The hypnosis trials had been complete failures. The sodium pentothal experiments had failed four times, and they'd only done that many because Lucky had insisted onit.

"They didn't fail, Lucky. They just showcased the fact that you really don't remember," Cooper told him now.

Lucky was due to be moved into his new apartment that afternoon. It was furnished, which was good since all he had was the small bag he'd brought from the Bain house. It was at his feet, the first time he'd seen it since he'd gotten here.

He imagined how carefully it had been gone over. Probably torn apart, X-rayed, sniffed by dogs and anything else they could think of doing.

"Hello, you there?" Cooper was waving a hand in front of his face.

"Sorry, yeah. Just thinking about the next steps."

"Let's focus back on you. You like to think ahead because it avoids focusing on you."

He hated it that Cooper knew that but supposed most people who dealt with him did. "Fine. I've got a couple of hours to kill."

Cooper shook his head. "Do you find Rex handsome?"

He nodded, like it didn't matter. But it did. Because Rex was hot and Lucky liked sex. Right now, that's all it was for Lucky—a could-be physical attraction that didn't get off the ground because, one, Rex had been the one to tell him who and what he was, and two, because Rex was happily with someone else. And Lucky wasn't the type of guy to fuck with someone he found attractive if they were in a relationship.

And when he told Cooper all of this, let it spill out since that's what he was supposed to do here, Cooper asked, "What scares you most about your past with Rex?"

Because Rex was all tied up in the horrific torture he'd faced. He wasn't the same man—neither was Rex. And Rex had moved on. Completely, it seemed.

Suppose I go back to that place and realize I still love him? And it's too late?

Fuck, he didn't want to have to deal with another disappointment. Now, with just a strong physical attraction and no knowledge of what had actually happened between them, it was so much easier.

Cooper was still watching him, waiting for the answer to his question.

"Everything," he said honestly. Cooper waited a beat and then bent to write something in the little notebook.

One day, Lucky was getting a look at the damned thing. Could only imagine the things Cooper was saying.

"You have another lie detector test. Then back to me, and then you can head down the block to your new place. You've got to check in with me twice a day, outside of our daily meetings."

"Still daily, huh?"

"For now. For your own good, Lucky."

Lucky nodded. Left his bag and went down the hall,

where he sat down in the familiar room to take what must've been his hundredth lie detector test since he'd arrived in Virginia. The man who administered the test placed the electrodes on Lucky while he made that kind of calming, I'm-your-friend small talk meant to make the innocent calm and the guilty nervous as hell.

Lucky just felt impatient. It didn't matter what questions they asked him, because the answers would always be the same.

The problem with these tests were that they were yes-or-no based. And Lucky couldn't answer some of the questions with either yes or no, because he didn't remember enough. He guessed the point was to throw questions at him like so many tennis balls across the net until he either fumbled or hit one they hadn't thought he'd be able to.

So far, that hadn't happened. What it did prove, he hoped, was that he was telling the truth about how he felt about Emme and the Bains.

He'd told Cooper he'd slept with Dash. He told him that he knew Dash was involved in this but didn't know how—but that he knew he wasn't Navy.

He told Cooper that he'd developed feelings for the man, faster than he'd thought possible. Because fuck it, he was going to be as honest as he could be. If it got Dash in trouble, that wasn't his problem.

He thought about his months here. He'd worked out. Read. Sat around. Saw various doctors. Saw more pictures of his brain than he'd ever wanted to.

Since he wasn't lying, he guessed all of this was easier. And everyone became nicer to him the more time that went by.

"We're going to try something different," Cooper told him when he walked back in after the test.

"We're going out to lunch?"

Cooper gave a sardonic grin as he popped a CD into his computer. "You passed the test, by the way. Again."

"Great. Is porn my reward?"

"You really are a fucking smartass," Cooper told him, pointed to the computer. Turned out he was playing a DVD but it wasn't porn.

It was him. Well, Josh, sitting at a table very much like the one Lucky had just left, with those familiar electrodes strapped to him.

"It's a video of you taking a lie detector test. Maybe two years before you were captured," Cooper clarified for him.

Lucky wondered why he'd waited to do this until now, but he guessed they wanted the element of surprise. And so he watched himself—the man he used to be—being prepped to take a lie detector test on the screen. The man he saw was a younger, more relaxed version of himself. His hair was longer and he had a beard.

"That was allowed," Cooper told him. "You were a longhair. It was encouraged."

He ran his hand through his hair now, then stopped

because Josh was doing the exact same thing on the screen.

It was weird watching you mirror you, when you had no memory of any of it.

"It's like watching a stranger," he whispered, more to himself than to Cooper.

The questions started off relatively simple. The man giving the test explained to Josh that they always started out with easy yes-or-no questions so they had a baseline for how the person reacted during a truth so they could easily spot a lie. It was the exact speech the man administering Lucky's tests had said to him every time.

"Josh, is your first name Josiah?"

"No."

"He's lying and the test isn't registering," Lucky said.

"You're lying," Cooper corrected.

"You're a Navy SEAL."

"No."

Josh the SEAL wasn't even blinking. Lying. Passing. "I was that good."

"Are you still?"

Lucky shook his head. "I'm guessing being a good liar's something you're born with. But this... Josh... he's enjoying himself. He's relaxed when he's lying. That's his tell." He glanced up at Cooper, who gave him an odd smile that didn't quite reach his eyes.

"You're right. I've been watching your old training tapes. Watching you. Looking for that goddamned tell. And I haven't seen ityet."

"What're you saying, Cooper? I've forgotten how to lie?"

"Have you?"

The tapes might be able to clear him—or Cooper could simply point out that Lucky was lying about not knowing how to lie. This all began to feel so goddamned impossible.

The tape went on for an hour. Several different tests on different days and Lucky watched himself beating the lie detector test. Every single time. He studied his movements on the screen, his eyes, looked for any little twitch or eyebrow wiggle.

There was nothing. Nothing, except for Josh's completely relaxed attitude, even as he remained friendly and professional to the man administering the test.

"I don't fucking understand that," he said, heard the anger in his voice and wasn't sure where it was coming from. "Only people who are psychotic can beat that. Unless I'm wearing something that throws it off…"

"You're not."

"Then I'm fucking psychotic," he muttered.

"No, Lucky, you're not. You were trained to beat lie detectors. Your body language tells lies. What the terrorists did to you was virtually the same thing—they forced you to believe the lies. It's how the CIA and Special Forces train their operatives to beat lie detector tests."

Cooper almost sounded sad, and Lucky knew how he felt.

They forced you to believe the lies.

Was he believing his own lies now, believing that he didn't have any memories when he really did?

Was he simply a product of his own training? A warning?

"I don't want to watch this anymore."

"That's not an option you have."

Lucky frowned, rubbed his palms against each other, then entwined and twisted his fingers together so hard that he swore they could break. But it was better than throwing the computer against the wall and getting shoved back in the small, windowless room again.

Dash had followed Lucky for several blocks. He found it easy to keep an eye on him. Probably too damned easy. Take a man whose life was once hand-to-hand combat and mix him with a healthy dose of suspicion coupled with amnesia and that was Lucky, who slammed him against the wall of the alleyway and held him there easily.

"If you wanted to fuck again, could've just asked." Dash's attempt at humor fell flat. Lucky pushed off of him and the wall simultaneously and started to walk away, the bag he'd left Africa with over his shoulder. "Lucky, come on."

Lucky turned. He didn't look especially angry—more like resigned when he told Dash, "You ruined my life and then disappeared. Sounds like that's your specialty."

"You've been talking to Emme."

"No, actually I'm not allowed to talk to Emme. I'm barely allowed to breathe fresh fucking air without a bodyguard and honestly, I'm shocked I'm allowed out to be on my own. I'm shocked they let me walk here by myself. Or did they? Is that what the hell you are—my bodyguard? My newest jailer?"

"No," Dash lied.

"Then why the hell are you here?" Lucky demanded. "Don't tell me you felt guilty."

"I had some business in the area." The lie bugged the shit out of his conscience. He'd thought himself long rid of it, but it popped up at the most inconvenient times.

Lucky wasn't buying it, not for a second. The man might not remember his SEAL training but those instincts that had gotten him this far never went away. He raised his brows and frowned. Muttered something about assholes who sleep with people so they can interrogate them and then try to give some lame-ass apology.

And then he walked away.

What did you expect, a welcome wagon? You literally fucked him over.

"Lucky, wait—"

"My name's Josiah. Or haven't you heard?"

"I heard. But I like Lucky better."

"Why? Because he's easy?"

"There's nothing about you that's easy, memory or no

memory," Dash said seriously.

Lucky processed that for a long moment and then said, "Are you hungry?"

"I could eat."

"Good, because you're buying."

Dash shook his head but followed the man into the street and walked next to him down the block to the diner. They took a booth in the back, and Lucky immediately slid into the seat with his back against the wall. Dash sat next to him so his back could be against a wall too.

What a fucking pair the two of them were.

They ordered—Lucky enough to feed a small country and Dash just said, "Double that" to the waitress because he didn't feel like wasting time figuring out food choices.

"Is your family all right?"

"Yes. They're fine."

"Do you have people there protecting them?" Lucky asked, and then his expression tightened. "Forget it. You can't tell me shit like that."

"They're protected. They're worried about you. That's pretty much the only reason Emme calls me, to make sure you're okay. She's pissed as hell at me."

Lucky's brow furrowed. "I didn't want to get between you and your family."

"I know."

"Why are you here, Dash?" Lucky asked again, his eyes boring into Dash's. "This isn't coincidence."

What did he have to lose by sharing? "I'm supposed to keep an eye on you."

"Why didn't they just tell me that?"

"I don't know how many people knew."

Lucky nodded. Drank some of the iced tea the waitress put down before he said, "Is this a trap, the whole letting me be on my own?"

"They don't know what else to do with you."

"Join the club." He leaned back in his chair. "You know I still have to meet with the shrink twice a day. And check in three times a day. I'm sure there's some kind of system set up in my new quarters that lets them know I'm inside, safely away from society."

"Lucky, they're torn between treating you like a criminal and a hero."

"Maybe there's always a fine line between the two."

Their food came. The waitress could barely fit all the plates on the table, smiled and said, "If you clean these, dessert's on the house."

Lucky seemed to take that as a personal challenge as he dug in. Dash slowly fixed his sandwich and asked, "So what's the shrink working on with you—still trying to get your memory back?"

"Some of that. He's also trying to get me to figure out why I pretended I never lost it." He took a bite of his sandwich and washed it down with the cold soda. "Personally, I think that's the most normal thing to do in this case."

"Why's that?"

"You've seen the scars. Who the hell would want to know how it happened? If you can get away scot free, with no nightmares…" He shook his head. "Rex has nightmares. Less now, he says, but I think he's lying. And Cooper—the shrink—says that he's worried all of this will come back to bite me in the ass someday, so it's better to try to get my memories back in a controlled environment. And since the Navy's still in charge of me, I don't have any other choice but to try."

"Now that's not true—the choice part, anyway."

Lucky ignored that, kept eating methodically. His table manners were impeccable, and he seemed to enjoy the food, which made Dash relax.

Lucky was taking all of this better than he'd ever expected. Was that because he was truly innocent? No reason to stress over something you didn't do—or couldn't remember you did.

16

Dash suspected they both knew what would happen when they walked through the door of Lucky's place, and he wasn't disappointed. He'd barely let Lucky get the door shut before he was on him, pinning him to the wall like he had the first time.

Lucky let the bag fall off his shoulder, kicked his shoes off, helped Dash yank down his jeans, all while never breaking the kiss.

Finally, Lucky was naked, putting his hands around the back of Dash's neck as if he could somehow pull him closer than he already was. "I fucking missed you," he murmured against Dash's mouth, and he didn't seem to require an answer since he went back to taking Dash's kisses.

He didn't need reassurances, Dash realized. He knew what he wanted, what he liked, who he liked. And he wasn't afraid to say it.

Dash had been right to fall for this man. Wanted to savor Lucky, but neither of them would last this first time. This would be quick and dirty, and then Dash would take his time with the man he'd been dreaming about for months.

"Please tell me you have lube," Lucky asked.

"Would you be insulted if I came prepared?"

"More insulted if you didn't."

"Good." He liberated it from his jacket pocket and Lucky helped pull his jeans down.

Lucky was climbing him then, not giving him a chance to get his shoes off.

Finally, he pushed inside Lucky, and Lucky hung onto him, flexing his hips to meet Dash's strokes. The man was so goddamned strong and this felt so right. Like coming home.

He wanted to bring Lucky back home to South Africa. Lucky, who fell asleep after he dragged him, still naked, onto the bed. He cleaned them up, which woke Lucky.

Lucky pulled him back down into bed, but he seemed restless now. Dash slung a leg over his to keep him in place, said, "I've been in Virginia since three days after you got here."

Lucky stared at him. "Why?"

"For you."

Lucky let out a short laugh. "To make sure I didn't escape?"

"To be here when they did let you out. To make sure you were okay."

"You didn't come to see me."

"I saw you, Lucky."

"They taped my hypnosis sessions and stuff, didn't they?" he muttered. "You got to watch all of that."

"Yes. Not your private sessions, though. Those are between you and your shrink." He reached down, rooted for his jacket and pulled out a pack of cigarettes. They were brand new. He also had the receipt that he showed Lucky. "I only have these after I have sex."

Lucky raised a brow. "You bought them four days after I got here."

"Right. And if we keep this up, I'm going to have to find a new reward for post-sex." He lit it, and after he took a long drag, Lucky took it and placed it in between his lips. The smoke drifted around him, and when he exhaled, he looked so fucking sensuous. Mysterious and brooding and everything Dash thought he'd never want in a guy.

He'd figured the best guy for him would be one who was straight forward, with zero secrets. Nothing to hide.

Instead, he'd fallen for a guy with everything to hide—a man who might've been turned by terrorists and who'd been dumped near Dash's family.

We can still get to you.

The message had been delivered to his family but had thankfully been intercepted by the bodyguards watching them. Lucky had still been on lockdown when it had come through. It would've been nearly impossible for him to get that message out.

But not impossible for the men who'd captured them to

let it serve as a warning. Which meant that Lucky was in as much danger as Dash and his family was. And that was something none of them had ever really considered. They'd been so wrapped up in proving Lucky had amnesia that they forgot they might not be the only ones who wanted to test him.

Lucky hadn't once asked what Dash was, although he had to have his suspicions. He knew he was a job to Dash, but he didn't know how Dash fit into all of this.

When and how Dash told him—if Dash ever told him—was left up to him. His last card to play. The one wall he had left between them.

Dash wasn't ready to let it crumble yet. But he would protect Lucky with everything he had.

"Where'd you go?" Lucky asked, handing him back the cigarette. He didn't look upset or pissed that Dash wasn't paying complete attention to him. At this point, most guys Dash had been with would be sulking or storming out.

"Still here."

In contented silence, they both lay against the pillows, sharing the cigarette and the quiet. At one point, Lucky picked up one of the books Dash had brought him and flipped through, starting to read somewhere in the middle. Dash stared at the patterned shadows the lights made on the walls and wondered what the next steps were, where his job would lead him next.

Where he wanted to *go* next. And that was something he

hadn't taken into consideration in many years.

Lucky was grateful as hell that he was here, out of the psych ward, maybe a step closer to being free.

Or maybe not. He shifted so he was on his side, facing Dash. Dash put out the cigarette and tossed the pack onto the nightstand. "This place isn't half bad."

Lucky snorted. It was a step up from the single room he'd been in, but it was nonetheless still a prison.

"I lived with your family for four years and you really didn't know anything about me? Had no clue I was there?"

"They didn't mention you," Dash said shortly and Lucky felt like he'd been punched. "It's not like that, Luck. They didn't say anything because they know I'm the suspicious type. Figured I'd have a fit they invited a stranger to live in my place."

"They didn't know what you really do."

"No. For their own safety. It's why I stayed away from them. Didn't want to bring those men around them. Had no goddamned idea the person I was searching for was there the whole time. I mean, shit like what happened to you is usually reported to the papers. The police. There's no trail of your rescue."

"Yeah, your family was very protective of me."

"The most fucking ironic thing I've ever heard," Dash

muttered.

Lucky shifted out from under Dash's body. "Want something to drink?"

They'd stopped at a market before coming to the apartment, where Lucky had bought some of the essentials. Correction—Dash paid for some of the essentials because Lucky had no cash.

"Sure."

He went to the small kitchen and grabbed a couple of bottles of water. He'd be staying here for God knew how long. Spartan furnishings, but there was space—a kitchen, living room, bedroom and bathroom. Small balcony. And no one to come in every night to check on him.

"Hey. Everything all right?" Dash was leaning against the doorjamb, watching him.

And no, it suddenly wasn't. Hadn't been but he wasn't sure why, couldn't put words to it.

Everything felt so strange. He didn't even know how he was supposed to get cash. Everything felt like it was closing in on him. Was this what Cooper wanted—was he waiting to see if the stress of this situation would cause him to crumble? "I need to pay you back for the groceries."

"No, you don't."

He stared at Dash's bare chest. He'd pulled on his jeans but left them unbuttoned, and Lucky, who never cared about being naked, suddenly felt vulnerable as hell. "What about next time I need food? How the fuck am I supposed to do that? Or are you my bodyguard and ATM card too?"

Dash frowned, pushed off the doorjamb and came toward him. Repeated, "What's wrong?"

He didn't know how to answer that. "Everything," came out, and Dash put a hand on the back of his neck and pulled his head down to his shoulder. Lucky rested it there, trying to breathe.

"It's okay."

"It's not, Dash. So fucking far from that," he whispered, not wanting to look Dash in the eye. "I watched a tape of me—Josh—today. I was taking a lie detector test. Lots of them. And I was lying and passing, lying and passing. Like it was nothing. I'm a trained liar."

"Yes."

He picked his head up in surprise at the complete non-judgment in Dash's tone. "You're okay with that?"

"I'm a trained liar too, Lucky. It's called survival. It's necessary for the jobs we do. Doesn't make you a bad person. In fact, it makes you better able to spot complete bullshit."

"Which is why you're here with me? Because you believe me?"

Dash smiled without hesitation, a soft smile that made his face look younger and more relaxed. "Yes. I believe you."

As much as Lucky wanted to believe that—and he did, deep in his heart—he couldn't shake the fact that Dash had admitted to being a trained liar too. Did Lucky remember enough about reading people to read this correctly?

"All you have to do is look in here." Dash pointed to Lucky's heart. "That's your best judge of anything."

"People get broken hearts all the time."

"What's that saying? Better to have loved and lost then to never have loved at all?"

Lucky remembered sitting up for several nights in a row with Emme, when she was crying about the asshole who'd ultimately broken her heart last year. She'd sobbed so hard he swore she'd break something and he'd hated that helpless feeling of not being able to do anything for her.

When he'd told her that, she'd wiped her tears and said, "But you are doing something, Luck. You're here."

Four months later, she'd gone on a blind date. He remembered telling her how much he admired her for that. "But aren't you scared it's going to happen all over again?"

"Of course. I guess that's part of the thrill. You liked the way the good parts made you feel, so you know it's something you want again."

But with no memories, he didn't know good from bad in his past.

But he did know good in his present—that was the Bains. And Dash and even Rex, Nate and Uncle. They'd all come to his rescue, stayed by his side.

"I don't want to let anyone down," he said now. "Suppose we find out that it's true, that they did break me…"

"None of that would be your fault, Lucky. The human

spirit can only endure so much. And did you ever stop to think that maybe your memory went because you willed yourself not to be turned? Maybe you were strong enough to know that you didn't want to do what those men were asking. The mind will shut down to protect you, knows what you can handle. Maybe, in this case, your mind's smarter than all of us who are trying to break into it."

"What's going on here, Dash? Between you and me, what the hell's really going on? Is it more than just sleeping together?"

"Yes."

"But it started out as a job for you. So how many others have you slept with for the job?"

"Are you only counting the men?"

"What do you think?"

"I think a smart man would find a way to avoid this conversation." Lucky snorted. "So it's a lot then."

"Yeah, it is. You learn a lot about a person when their defenses are down. Sex is the best at that."

"Doesn't that mean your defenses are down too?"

"What do I really have to hide? I'm seeking information and they think the reason is because I'm interested in them. And I am." He locked his eyes to Lucky's. "With you, I was interested in you beyond the job. I know how lame it sounds to say we connected that first night, but I dare you to argue otherwise."

"I'm not denying it," Lucky told him.

"That's why you weren't completely pissed at me."

"I was pissed. But I wanted to prove that I'd never hurt you or your family."

"So we're really doing this," Dash said, more to himself than to Lucky.

"I guess we are. Yeah."

17

Things were slowly returning to normal for Rex and Sawyer, although Rex realized that neither man wanted their old normal. They were both ready to stretch, and Rex knew that Sawyer had been right when he'd said they didn't know each other well.

It was all sex and work, work and sex. It was time to dig deeper. There was no choice. So while he and Sawyer ate Chinese takeout from the cartons in the living room and Rex told him about seeing Lucky, about how Lucky had been released to an apartment but would continue with his therapy sessions, Sawyer seemed more atease.

"I'd like you to meet him," Rex said. "He wants to meet you."

"Yeah, I'd like that." Sawyer wound some noodles around his fork. "We've got tomorrow night off."

"I was thinking we could spend some time on my boat."

"You have a boat?" Sawyer asked stupidly.

Rex nodded. "Just got her ready for the season."

"I go back and forth between liking not knowing

everything about you and worrying that we missed some big steps," Sawyer muttered and stood. He grabbed some of the empty containers to bring to the garbage, but Rex stopped him, saying, "Sawyer, we save each other's lives. We know what each of us will do under the worst conditions. We're closer than most people get in a lifetime."

"Doesn't mean I don't want to know what you like to do."

"Besides you?"

"Can you be serious?"

"Fine. I fish."

"Okay, so let's go."

"Do you fish?"

"For me to know and you to find out," Sawyer said as he went into the kitchen. "You sound like you're two," Rex called after him.

Sawyer knew how to fish. Or at least, Rex assumed he did, based on the way he threaded the lines, hooked the bait and tackle and rigged the lines.

"Let me guess—you did this off a yacht?" Rex asked him as he steered through the marina and headed out into the ocean just before sundown.

"No," Sawyer corrected with a smirk, then added, "But we did travel on the yacht for a few summers."

Rex nuzzled his neck. "You were yachting. I was cleaning

fish for rich guys like you."

Sawyer reached back and rubbed his head. "Betcha all the rich guys hit on you."

"I did all right."

After an hour of travel, Rex stopped in one of his favorite spots, near a cove that was secluded plus a great spot for fishing.

As for Sawyer, the water was a second home to him, and he wasn't to be deterred from taking dives off the boat even before Rex got them to their destination. He swam along next to the boat for some of the trip, like a puppy who needed to work off his energy before he could relax.

"This is great," Sawyer said now as he climbed back into the boat, naked and dripping wet.

"Would've taken you out here a lot sooner if I'd known I'd be getting a show."

Sawyer smirked but made no move to towel off. "You have too many clothes on."

"Agreed."

Rex undid his cargos, but instead of taking them off, he sat with his pants open and motioned for Sawyer to come closer. "Climb on."

Sawyer did as Rex told him as Rex popped open the lube he'd grabbed from his pocket. He reached around Sawyer and fingered him as the man groaned and pushed back against his fingers.

Darkness covered them. Coupled with the lights on the

boat that wouldn't allow anyone to see in without being pulled up right next to them, they were shielded from any prying eyes that might come by.

"I hope we don't get arrested for this," Rex said.

"Sex is allowed in open water."

"Not a free show."

No one was around, but Sawyer didn't seem concerned at all. He pushed Rex's hand away and grabbed Rex's cock instead. Angled it and pushed his body down over Rex's cock, slowly, so fucking slowly that Rex thought he'd lose his mind. But this was his show, so Rex watched Sawyer's face until he was balls-deep inside him.

"Beautiful boy," he murmured.

"Ah, he falls back on Dom terminology," Sawyer said, then moaned when Rex angled his hips and drove himself in deeper.

"You seem to like it."

"Yeah." Sawyer put his hands on either side of the railing behind him and moved up and down. Kissed Rex. Moaned against his mouth. He lost track of time, of everything except the way Sawyer's body moved against his.

A slow shudder of release happened for Sawyer first. He looked surprised as hell that it snuck up on him. "Fuck, Rex."

Rex grabbed his hips and thrust up several times before his own orgasm blinded him. Sawyer grabbed him, held him tight as they both continued to shudder through the aftershocks.

When Sawyer moved back, Rex took his T-shirt off and used it to wipe the rest of Sawyer's come off the man's belly and chest. Sawyer grinned unrepentantly.

"Don't fish naked," Rex advised.

Sawyer climbed off him. "Jesus, my legs are like jelly."

Rex stood, snaked an arm around Sawyer's waist as Sawyer pulled his shorts on. Held him for longer than he needed to, because it felt damned good. Better than it had in a long time. Sawyer learned against him and the sound of the water lapping the boat lulled them into nearly sleeping on theirfeet.

Hell, they'd both had experience in that.

Finally, Rex went and set up the lines and they fished blues until close to midnight. Did the whole catch and release thing for all of them.

This was what they'd needed, time together, space from work. Time apart from the rabid need for sex that always grabbed them, because they never seemed to have enough time together.

"Who taught you to fish?" Rex asked.

"My dad. He was Navy. He died when I was five."

"Accident?"

Sawyer looked straight ahead at the ocean when he said, "Yes. He drowned. Took his speedboat out during a storm, because he loved storms."

"Sawyer…"

"And before you say anything, I'm obviously okay on boats, Rex. I joined the fucking Navy."

Rex rubbed a hand along the back of Sawyer's neck. "It was still hard on you."

"Yeah, it was. I don't remember much, but I remember time on the boat with him.

Not the yacht or the speedboat, but a dinky little fishing boat he'd row out onto the lake near our house. After he died, mom got rid of it. I guess she thought it would make her grief easier. And then I got sick."

Rex's insides froze. He tried to keep his voice as normal as possible when he said, "Sick?"

"Yeah, leukemia. Went into remission when I was six," he said. "I'd been clear for twelve years when I enlisted, so I was able to get a waiver."

"And you get checked for it regularly?"

"Yeah, Doc checks for me," Sawyer said quietly.

"And everything's okay?" he asked, surprised how calm he sounded because he swore his heart nearly dropped to the fucking ground.

"It's fine, yes. Tests just came back yesterday. All clear still."

"I'm glad you told me."

"I didn't want to freak you out."

"I'm trying not to," Rex admitted. "But it's better that I know."

Sawyer looked like he had something else to tell him.

"It kind of runs in my family. Skipped my dad but my grandfather…same thing happened. Only his came back when he was an adult."

"How old was he when it came back?"

"Twenty-eight."

Sawyer's age. Jesus Christ. "I'm guessing you left that bit of family history out when the Navy asked?"

"*I* didn't know, Rex. At the time I enlisted, I didn't know, so yeah, I left it out." His voice sounded raw. "My mom didn't want it hanging over my head and my grandfather died long before I was born—his medical records are somewhere in Europe. She thought I'd been through too much. And she figured that I shouldn't spend all that time worrying about it. When I was younger, she kept bringing me for tests and she knew I'd have to be in the Navy so…"

"When did she tell you?"

"She never did. My stepdad finally did, about two years ago. He thought I had a right to know."

"What do you think?"

"It's not the reason I'm angry with my mom. You know what bothers me about her, but at the same time, I understand. She loved Dad. Couldn't get over it." He sighed. "I would've worried the entire time I knew. I almost wish my stepfather didn't tell me."

Rex tried to keep calm, because he understood what Sawyer was saying—there was no good choice there. "Like you said, you get tested. They didn't have the same advances then as they do now."

"Right," Sawyer said firmly.

"Come here." Rex put the line down. Sawyer did too and Rex just held him tight for a long time.

"Not how I wanted to tell you," Sawyer said. "Didn't want to ruin the first night we've both been able to get away from all the shit."

"Doesn't matter. I don't want to get away from anything that has to do with you, understand?"

Sawyer nodded, and Rex held him tighter to make sure he did. "I wish we could stay out here all night."

"Your wish, my command," Rex told him, because he couldn't think of a better night to keep Sawyer all to himself, away from the reach of the world. "We can pull the inflatable mattress and sleep right out here, under the stars."

Sawyer finally smiled.

"Wait here. Let me fix everything." Rex was well aware of how badly he wanted those words to apply to everything in Sawyer's life. For tonight, he did what he could, got the mattress and blankets and radio and food, put everything near them. Anchored so they wouldn't drift too far out. And then he tucked Sawyer in next to him. The man shivered against him, the strain of the past obviously weighing heavily on him.

"Tell me what I can do to make it easier."

"Just knowing you know helps. I can tell Doc you can

check with him about my tests too."

"That would help me," Rex said. "But that's not what I asked."

Sawyer still looked so troubled. "When my dad drowned...he didn't die right away. The Coast Guard found him. Pulled him out and revived him, but he never really came back. They got his heart started but the docs determined he'd been under water for at least twenty minutes, based on his distress call. They were able to start his heart because the water was really cold and the medics at the scene were hoping that was enough to preserve brain function but he didn't have any DNR papers in place, and..."

They lived on the edge of life and death most of the time with their jobs, but this...

"Tell me what you want, baby."

"She kept my dad alive longer than he would've wanted. I was young, but I knew that. He was really active. I remember all the wires. She wouldn't let him go. Things got ugly with my mom because I talked to my gram about it later on, because I didn't understand why she'd let him suffer. And then later, after my mom got remarried, things got bad because my mom and my stepdad were always fighting."

Rex held him tighter. "We'll sign papers that detail exactly what you want. And if it kills me, I'll make sure they're followed to the letter. And we can look at the papers as a good-luck thing—if they're in place, means we'll never need them."

"Thanks," Sawyer said quietly. "I know we're not supposed to have that in place…"

Because they were never supposed to go into a mission thinking of their own mortality. That was a terrible mindset.

Some guys wrote a letter before every trip. Some didn't. But plans like this… "I'll make one too," Rex told him.

"You don't have to."

"Do I ever do shit I don't want to?"

"No."

"Then don't argue."

"Okay."

Rex stroked a hand through Sawyer's hair. "I know it couldn't have been easy telling me. Especially with what's happening with Josh—Lucky—but I don't want you to worry about us. I've got to help him. I know you understand that. But I'm not going back to him, Sawyer. You've got to believe me."

"I do, Rex. I think my issues were way more about us than they ever were about him. But being with you like this…it makes me realize that it's okay that we still have a lot of learning about each other to do."

Rex slid a hand down to finger Sawyer's ass, watched the man smile and move against his hand as his fingers got more aggressive. "Still so goddamned tight."

Sawyer bit at Rex's shoulder as he added a second finger,

then a third. He urged Sawyer's leg up, hooked it over his shoulder as he continued to play with the younger man's ass. Sawyer groaned against Rex's chest, his breath warm, his body trembling as he fought to stay still after Rex added the fourth finger.

He wouldn't go further—not out here and not tonight, but seeing how responsive Sawyer was to just the mere suggestion of it made Rex put fisting on his list of things to try. And soon.

For now, he contented himself with turning his four fingers inside Sawyer as a unit, filling him, holding him captive so all he could do was take what Rex gave him. His body had stilled, even without Rex telling him to. The look in Sawyer's eyes was a mix of lust and peace, and he continued, keeping Sawyer in his semi-trance, not letting him rub his cock against Rex.

Finally, he could tell Sawyer was growing desperate, but it was such a goddamned good desperate. He whimpered. His neck corded.

"You can come from this—not letting you touch your cock."

"Fuck. Rex." Sawyer's words were barely a breath.

"Come on, baby. Come for me." Rex eased his fingers out, then slid one back in with his knuckle folded to brush Sawyer's prostate with a light tap. Sawyer stiffened with that, and Rex hit his gland harder, several times quickly, and Sawyer came, spilling his come between their bodies.

After that, Sawyer slept while Rex held him and watched the stars. He didn't wake the man up even when he piloted the boat back before dawn, but Sawyer stretched and rose just in time to see the sun come up.

18

The next morning, Dash listened as Lucky checked in with Cooper, as per the agreement made for his release. They had breakfast and then Lucky went to meet Cooper for a therapy session.

Dash didn't see Lucky again until that afternoon at Lucky's apartment. The man looked drained. Slightly angry and a little defeated.

Dash hated seeing him like that. "Bad session?"

Lucky shrugged. "Don't want to talk about it. How's Emme?"

Dash had promised him that he'd call Emme and let her know Lucky was okay. "She's thrilled you're okay. She's still barely speaking to me."

Lucky looked like he wanted to say something, but he didn't. Not on that subject. Instead, he pointed to the two large boxes Dash had carried in and set on the floor. "What are those?"

"My photos. My work. You can look."

Lucky did, lifted the lids and pulled out a small stack of

pictures. That one was simply labeled *Chile*. "What're you doing with them?"

"I need you to organize them."

"You're giving me busy work now?"

"Do you have something better to do?"

"I could find something."

"That pays?"

Lucky smiled. "Cash only. Small bills."

Dash snorted with laughter. "Just don't fuck it up. Each job gets its own book."

"Any particular order?"

"Use your judgment. I'd like to see how the work speaks to you."

"You trust me with that?"

"Yeah," Dash said. "Besides, I can always change them around."

Lucky absently shot him the middle finger, but he was already sitting among the stacks of pictures, engrossed in Dash's trip to Chile.

"I'm going to head out for a little while—I've got a meeting to go to, okay?" Dash told him and Lucky barely nodded. Dash was grateful he was so caught up in the photography, because he didn't like what he'd planned for Lucky.

But he told himself it was necessary, for both their peace of mind. For Dash's family. The camera Dash had planted in Lucky's apartment would capture reactions. And he felt like shit for doing it, but he knew Lucky had no expectations of privacy. Had been told as much.

So Dash sat in his rented house in front of the computer with the camera feed and watched Lucky working with his photos.

Dash held his breath when Lucky got to the stack he'd been waiting for. Lucky had taken his time with the first two batches. Both places Lucky had been as a SEAL.

Lucky took an interest in them, although Cooper had told him that wasn't the right word. These places were a part of Lucky—he'd been drawn to Dash's photos from the start and ultimately Dash, because of that.

"So wait…the feelings he has for me…you're saying it might only be some kind of transference?" Dash had asked.

Cooper had shrugged.

"I fucking hate shrinks and their non-answer answers," he'd told the man.

Now, that conversation was etched in his mind as he watched Lucky begin to lay out the photos on the floor as he'd done with the others. It looked like a big puzzle he was trying to make sense of…

He sat back on his heels and stared. Like he'd done with the other pictures, he hadn't really looked at them until they were all laid out in front of him.

Lucky tilted his head as he stared, and Dash moved closer to the computer screen, looking for the recognition. A look of horror or satisfaction, the lift of a brow, a subtle change of expression. Anything.

But Lucky looked no different than he had when perusing the other photos. A look of appreciation, a look of frustration that maybe this scratched the wall put up between his past and present…but it wasn't enough to slam through it. Not even close.

And if those pictures didn't do it…

He sat back and breathed out, frustrated. Dash's memories were coming to the surface all too easily and he hated it. He watched the pictures—how Lucky put them in an order Dash wouldn't have picked himself but he had to admit it worked better—and he could point to each picture and retrace hiss teps.

This is where Jim and I infiltrated.

This is where Jim and I got captured.

This is the last place I saw Jim alive.

The difference was, Dash had seen the body. Escaped with Jim's body bag…saw the DNA.

Twenty-four hours after Jim was killed, the SEAL team with Rex and Lucky had come in and Dash had escaped.

He'd seen Lucky's scars.

He had them too. He just wore them on the inside.

Dash accompanied Lucky to his afternoon therapy session. Cooper looked less than pleased, but Dash didn't give a shit.

"Hey Lucky, can you grab me a soda?" Cooper asked after the men had walked in. Lucky rolled his eyes. "If you want time alone to talk about me, could just say that," he called over his shoulder as he walked out.

"He really is a smartass," Cooper muttered. "And what the hell are you thinking, spending time with him like this?"

"You're not finding any evidence that he's a traitor. I like him, Cooper. If he's not a traitor, he's a decorated naval hero."

"That's true. But it's more complicated than that, and you know it. From all accounts, Josh Kent was an exemplary SEAL. Calm. Collected. Never showed violent tendencies. His testing from then and now, it's eerily similar. I can't see him suddenly turning violent, even if he remembers."

"But you're worried because he does have specialized training."

"Maybe. He seems to sense that. I've confirmed that he never used excessive force at his job. He's been briefed in that. It's been demonstrated to him in a controlled environment in case it triggered something. I was hoping it would."

"So nothing worked."

"Hypnosis was a bust. Drugging him was worse. Showing him the lie detector test tapes did nothing but upset him. Same with talking to Rex. The only thing I haven't done is recreate the torture. And I won't do that," Cooper said.

"Suppose I asked you to?" Dash turned to see Lucky holding three sodas as he strolled across the room. "Sorry, was I supposed to knock?"

"See, it's stuff like that—he remembers how to sneak up on people," Cooper muttered. "Doesn't even realize he's doing it."

"I knew what I was doing this time, Doctor," Lucky said.

"Forget it, Lucky," Dash told him. "We're not recreating the torture."

"Cooper said it might work."

"And as you've pointed out to me many times, why would you want to remember that torture? This is a specific kind of therapy. What you're talking about is barbaric. I won't do it—not even at a pretend level." Cooper put his hands on Lucky's shoulders, stared at him. "Remember, Lucky, there's no reason to go back there now."

After a long moment, Lucky jerked away from him and turned to Dash. "Then you do it."

Dash opened his mouth and then closed it. Lucky gave a small smile that didn't reach his eyes. "Guess that's not a no."

"Lucky—"

"I'm ready to start anytime. Set it up," he commanded.

"This isn't happening on my watch," Cooper said.

Dash turned away to face the window.

"If this is my last shot to prove that I didn't do anything

wrong, don't you think I have the right to choose if I'll take it or not?" he asked Dash.

"You want me to do something that might cause you PTSD—or worse. You're free, Lucky—" Dash started.

Lucky pulled at his shoulder so Dash was forced to face him again. "Free? Really?

Coming in here constantly for monitoring makes me free?"

"It could be worse," Dash said.

19

Lucky slammed out of Cooper's office. Dash didn't follow him and Lucky was half pissed and half glad about that.

Neither man would help him. Which meant Rex would probably refuse too and really, how could Lucky ask Rex to go through something he'd already survived, even if it was a simple simulation?

He didn't go back to the apartment—not right away. Maybe he was trying to see if Dash could really find him wherever he went, or maybe he wanted to worry him. But he spent the next couple of hours walking around, sitting in a park, watching kids play.

Did he ever do that? He pictured his background as a child like some deep, dark disturbing hole, with a definite lack of toys and laughter.

Talking about it with Rex had made him sad, and it made him want to know more. But the thing was, there were only so many things Rex could tell him. Rex hadn't lived it.

And you can't remember it.

He stayed until it was dark. Until his stomach growled.

Until he realized he missed two check-ins, and he wondered if they'd sent someone after him.

It was only when he stood to leave that he realized they had.

"How long have you been there?" he asked Dash as he passed him on his way out of the park.

"As long as you have."

"Fucker," Lucky muttered.

"You're coming with me."

"Where's that?"

"Just follow me to the goddamned car." Now Dash was angry and Lucky was pissed that he was.

A big circle of pissed off, that's what they were.

"Are you taking me back to Cooper?" he asked once he got inside the rental car.

"No." Dash gunned the car out of the parking lot next to the park and headed into an area Lucky didn't recognize at all.

"Then where?"

"You used to live in this area."

"So what? You want me to get more upset that I can't remember where I used to live?"

"If you want to." Dash pulled into a driveway and then a garage. He waited until it closed behind him before getting out of the car, and Lucky followed him.

He guessed this was Dash's house—a house he was renting, since it had none of the personality his apartment in South Africa did. "Why are we here?"

"Why not?" Dash asked.

Lucky felt his fists tighten involuntarily. He unclenched them just as fast, took a deep breath. "What do you want from me, Dash?"

Dash turned on him fiercely. "I want you to be angry. To give a shit."

"You think I don't give a shit?"

"No, I don't. You're all calm and cool. Everything's fine. You're all understanding. Nothing's a big deal. You ask me to fucking torture you like it's no bigger deal than buying you dinner."

"For you, I didn't think it would be."

Dash pressed his lips together, shook his head. Pointed at Lucky. "See, it's shit like that—that's how I know you're pissed, deep down."

Lucky wasn't about to tell him it wasn't nearly as deep down as he'd like it to be. "So you're going to push me to get angry? Like I'm the Hulk or something?"

"Go for it."

"No. You don't know what I'm capable of. Neither do I."

"And that's what this is all about." A statement rather than a question and Lucky guessed Dash saw through something even Lucky himself hadn't fully admitted to. At least not until right now.

"So what if it is? It's a legitimate concern. Even Cooper talked about it."

"Cooper said he didn't think you were violent. That even if you'd been holding back, you wouldn't have been able to hang onto a violent hair-trigger temper for four years and counting."

"Maybe no one's pissed me off enough."

"Then let me be the first." Dash paused. "Is that why you want to simulate the torture? That way if you lose it, you'll be in a controlled environment?"

"I want my memory back. I'll do whatever I have to in order to get it."

Dash slammed him, two hands on his chest, and Lucky went back and hit the wall.

Hard. He pushed off and headed for Dash, then stopped. "Go on. Do your worst."

"Fuck. You."

"Until you do it, you're never going to know if you can fight and still control yourself. Unless you're scared to find out you're not as tough as they say you were."

"You really think that's going to goad me into fighting you?"

"I hope so."

"What if I hurt you?"

"I've already hurt you," Dash whispered. "Come on, hurt me."

"So we'll be even."

"We'll never be even. Best I can hope for is you forgiving me."

Lucky swallowed, felt the anger rise. "Don't you give me that shit—that pity shit."

"I don't pity you. But I don't understand how you can be so fucking nice to me, after I turned you in. Why? I know you're pissed. I know you must feel betrayed. But all you've done is let me in further. Why?"

"Right now, I don't know."

"I see you trying to hold it in. You're never going to know what you're capable of unless you let it out. So take it out on me, Lucky. I can handle you. Always could."

He went for Dash. Tackled him to the ground. Dash used his weight against him and rolled them both until Lucky hit the back of the couch hard.

It forced Lucky off of Dash, and Dash used that opportunity to pin Lucky to the ground, a hand on his throat. Lucky smiled and when Dash frowned, he pushed up hard, knocking a surprised Dash over. And then they were up, circling each other. Lucky swung at Dash, connecting with his right cheekbone, and then he used a few fast uppercuts to get Dash in the solar plexus.

With Dash trying to catch his breath, he knocked the man's knees out from under him, pinned him, a forearm across his throat. He looked down into Dash's face and that's when he lost it.

Dash rolled him—Lucky would try to recreate it later, because it was a damned good move to know, but with zero luck—and Lucky ended up on his belly on the ground,

Dash on him with a stranglehold.

The fight went on like that for what seemed like forever, until they were both breathing hard. Lucky's lip was bleeding. Dash's jaw ached. Their clothes were torn, and neither man was a clear winner.

What was clear was that Dash could control him. And Lucky did have a measure of control that he seemed relieved by.

Dash ended up pinning Lucky to the floor, barely. Asked, "Do you forgive me?"

"What the fuck—shouldn't I be asking that about you?" Lucky gasped, looked confused.

"Think about it, Lucky. There was a reason you were in that jungle. Everything you've been through has been because of that. Everything happened because of those CIA agents. So I'm going to ask again—can you forgive me?"

Dash eased up on the grip, and Lucky turned onto his side, looked up into Dash's face and suddenly he knew exactly what the man was talking about. "You're not Navy."

"No," Dash whispered. "I know you were told what the mission was about."

"We were sent in to rescue two captured CIA agents." As soon as the words came out of Lucky's mouth, he knew he was looking at one of them. "One died. And one escaped. You're CIA."

"Yes."

"You're the agent who escaped."

Dash nodded. "It's my fault you don't have a memory. Even if you were turned, that would be on me."

"You weren't trying to get captured."

"No," Dash agreed. "But I pushed ahead on that mission, ignored my gut to turn back. I fucked my partner over, and then an entire SEAL team. I have to live with that, with every single consequence born of that. I didn't know the SEALs had been captured until they'd been released," he admitted. "I was hurt. Delirious. A local family found me passed out in their field, took me in. By the time I was healthy enough to track down a phone, I'd learned about the goatfuck that happened."

"Were you taken off the case?"

"Technically, yes. It was too dangerous to chase the men who'd captured me. And when they never seemed to make a move to find me or Rex or Nate or Uncle, the CIA kept looking. And since I didn't know if Rex, Nate or Uncle had been turned, I watched them. They were my best lead, because the terrorist who'd kidnapped us had gone underground, and I knew sussing him back out would take years."

"But you always believed I was alive."

"Always. But you managed to surprise the hell out of me, Lucky."

Dash wasn't sure how Lucky was going to react. He waited, held his breath, and while he saw a natural flood of emotions, it was clear that no memories had been triggered.

No anger either. Lucky brushed his bruised cheek gently as he asked, "All this time, you were actually looking for me?"

Dash didn't deny it. No point in hiding it any longer. "I spent most of the time following Nate, because he was more mobile than Uncle. Uncle stayed in one place, so he was easier to keep track of. But Nate rarely sat still, and that made us suspicious. And I stayed away from my home because I didn't know if he was hunting me just as much as I was hunting him."

"So you followed the guy you thought might be working for the men who tried to kill you."

"Yes."

"But Nate's showing up at the bar…that was all chance. He was just there to surf."

"Yes."

Lucky started. "Oh, fuck…you thought Nate might be going after your family."

Dash nodded. "But you were already there. Living with them."

Lucky shook his head like he was trying to process everything. "You must've been scared for them."

"Scared's one word. But when Nate found you and you had no clue what was going on, I had to make sure it wasn't an act. Maybe Nate knew I was on to him and you guys cooked up an amnesia plan."

"You thought I might be a terrorist. Someone who wanted to kill you."

"Yes."

"So you fucked me."

"I told you before, Lucky, it's part of my job. I needed you to open up and trust me." As soon as the words started coming out of his mouth, Dash wanted to pull them all back. But Lucky needed to know everything about him.

"Are you trying to be honest or are you hoping I'll get pissed and tell you to get the fuck out?"

"A little of both."

"What do you want me to say, Dash? That it hurts to know your fucking me was a job?"

"If you think that, then say it."

"I think it started that way. I think you wanted to believe that and yeah, you're a good liar. But you weren't one hundred percent acting that night. I think that's what you're the most freaked about."

Dash wanted to turn away, but he couldn't. The guy had no memories, but every single operator's instinct was there. His ability to read people was frightening.

Dash had met his match in more ways than training.

"Just answer me one question," Lucky said, didn't wait before continuing, "Are you most worried that you can never fully trust that I'm not plotting to turn you into that terrorist?"

"I could let that worry me, Lucky. Not going to lie. Unfortunately, in my line of work, everyone I know's trying to do that."

"You're as lonely as I am," Lucky said.

Dash could only nod. "Been lonely for a long time, but I never forced a relationship because of it."

"How long were you captured for?" Lucky asked.

Dash knew how many days the SEALs were captured for. Josh Kent's number was always slightly shorter, but now, it looked like he'd probably been held the longest of all of them.

"Three days," Dash said, feeling so incredibly stupid for saying so. Three days to the months and months of torture Lucky and his team had endured.

But Lucky, fucking incredible man that he was, took Dash's face in his hands and told him, "This isn't a contest. One hour's still long enough to fuck you up. But you can't let it, because then they win."

He blinked at the simple truth behind Lucky's words. For years, the man sitting next to him had been his goal. Now, that objective was met, mission complete and he was lost.

He didn't know what he'd expected, that Lucky would admit he'd been tortured. Because Lucky had nothing to do with Jim's death and everything to do with Dash's escape. He owed Lucky his life—literally—and for the past four years, he'd taken it upon himself to hunt Lucky down like a dog and charge him and his team with treason.

Now, that man was here—no evidence of treason. No memories...and Dash didn't know what the fuck he was supposed to do next.

When he told Lucky that last part, Lucky said, "I can take care of that. Let me."

And Dash did, watched Lucky strip and then let Lucky strip him. Pin his arms above his head. "You really don't give me credit for anything, Dash."

"I knew you suspected..."

"From like day one—at least when Rex showed. I figured, what were the chances of you being so invested in this?" Lucky bent down and bit one of Dash's nipples lightly, but still enough to make Dash gasp. "But I'm patient. Figured you had your reasons, just like I had mine for trying to stay so mellow."

He bit the other nipple, then licked it, sucked it, until Dash was pressing his hips up, trying to grind his cock into Lucky's belly. "But now, our reasons are out. And we're in the same place we were that first night. And I'm thinking that's a good thing, right?"

"Right."

He felt Lucky's cock enter him and he grabbed onto the man's biceps. Lucky didn't let up, pushed into him slowly, so fucking slowly. And this was far less an act of dominance than it was allowing Dash to let go. Of his guilt. His anger and shame. Let go of everything, because Lucky had him.

"Not letting go," Lucky told him. "Life's too short. If anyone knows that now, I do."

Dash buried his face in Lucky's shoulder, letting the man take him, pumping hard until Dash was flying, then breaking into a thousand pieces with his climax.

Lucky was there. *Putting me back together.*

"We'll put each other back together. Doesn't matter if it takes a lifetime," Lucky told him.

It wasn't until then that Dash realized he'd spoken the words out loud.

Later, in Dash's arms, Lucky let his fears out in the dark because they seemed less real that way.

"My whole life needs to be rebuilt. How can you rebuild a man's entire past?"

"I don't think you can."

"Then what do I do?"

"You keep moving forward. And this is the past you'll remember. So let's try to make it really damned good," Dash told him.

"What if…"

"You can't remember it."

"What if the memories come back and all I remember is the brainwashing? Maybe I'm just going to snap to

converted."

"That could never happen. You're not going to forget all of this…"

"Suppose I do? If I remember…" He stopped. "Who am I kidding? I'm the Navy's bitch, no matter what."

"They can't keep you forever, Lucky. At this point, it's more for your protection."

"I don't need their protection."

"You need someone's," Dash told him. "You need mine."

"So you'd be my keeper."

"Not like I wouldn't be around you anyway."

Lucky stared. "I'd have to choose to believe that was true."

"Then start believing."

20

"Lucky!" Emme yelled into the phone so loudly that Lucky was pretty sure she shattered his eardrum.

And he didn't care. Hearing her voice was exactly what he needed. "Hey, Em."

"Should I...can I still call you Lucky?" she asked hesitantly.

"That's the only name I go by," he told her.

"So I guess you still don't remember anything. I was hoping maybe...I don't know what I was hoping. Just that you were okay. That no one was hurting you."

"No one is, Em. The Navy has to do its job."

"Right. The Navy and Dash."

She sounded angry at her brother, and that was the last thing he wanted to happen. "He's doing his job. Protecting you."

"I can't believe you can defend him after everything. He ruins your life and then he just disappears, like he always does."

Obviously, Dash hadn't told her that he was here in

Virginia. And although Lucky knew he probably shouldn't give away that information, he also realized that repairing the relationship of the brother and sister was more important. "He's here, Em. Dash is here."

There was a pause of surprise and then she asked, "What? I knew he'd been checking up on you but I thought he meant by phone and through his contacts…"

"He's here *with* me," he said. "What do you mean, with you?"

"He's ah…I don't think it started out that way. I mean, it might've. He came here to check on me. And then, when they let me out of the brig—"

"He put you in jail?"

"The Navy did. Come on, Em. You've got to understand. And Dash's staying here with me. He's trying to help."

"You're still sleeping with him."

"Yes."

"I'll never understand men," she muttered.

"You understand us better than we do ourselves," he told her. "I really miss you."

"God, I miss you too, Luck. Do you think…will you be able to come back here?"

"I don't know. I really don't."

"Will I be able to visit you?" she asked.

"I don't see why not. But probably not anytime soon."

"For the record, I know you could never hurt us, not me or Mom and Dad. Although I wouldn't mind if you

punched Dash for me."

He laughed at that. He thought about all Emme didn't know about Dash, about how his capture was what brought Lucky to him in the first place, that it started a chain of events that would reverberate through their lives and never stop. But that wasn't his story to tell. Might never be. "Don't be too hard on him. He's been good to me."

"I hate it that I can't trust his motives anymore."

"Yeah, well, I do."

"Were you really a SEAL? I mean, that's pretty cool. I can see why coming back and bartending might not be so exciting."

"Sounds like the best job in the world still," he told her honestly. He looked up and saw Dash coming in the door. "I've got to go, Em. But I'll call soon."

"Yes, you will," she told him. "I'm so glad you're okay, Lucky."

"Yeah, me too." He hung up the phone and admitted, "I told her you were here. With me. Why didn't you tell her?"

"She's so pissed at me. What the hell would it change?"

"She wants me to punch you."

"Go for it. I want to punch me too half the time." Dash smiled, then pointed to the cameras that were on the counters. "Want to go take some pictures with me?"

"Is this some new form of therapy?"

"It's just picture-taking, Lucky."

Even though Lucky didn't fully buy that, he went anyway.

Dash walked with Lucky along the beach, noted that Lucky didn't hesitate near the water.

Anyone who'd experienced a near drowning probably should've. But his body's instincts, all that water training, had kicked in and saved him. He was too brave to be scared of the water.

"It was hard the first few times," Lucky said with a sideways glance at him. "You're thinking about me and the water."

"Didn't realize I was that obvious."

"Yeah, well, I'm guessing I know you better than most. No matter how much you tried not to let that happen."

Dash frowned.

"Anyway, yeah, the water thing freaked me, but I knew I had to get over it, and fast, since I was going to be living and working on a beach. So I went in one night—"

"Night?"

"Because no one would be around to see me freak out."

"Or die. Or get eaten by sharks," Dash pointed out. "You are so much like your sister."

"My sister worries too much, so I'm guessing that's not a compliment."

"Your sister worries about the people she cares about," Lucky corrected. "So definitely a compliment."

"Fuck, this is complicated."

Lucky answered by grabbing one of the cameras and starting to shoot the ocean. Dash followed suit, because this, at least, was uncomplicated, and the two of them were caught between the clicking sounds of the cameras and the loud stir of th eocean.They were the only two on the beach—the afternoon had darkened and clouds had begun to rush in, a rolling burst of angry gray that threatened to break over them. A force of nature, just the way Lucky had been trained to be.

Lucky, who'd lost himself in the act of picture-taking. It was the way Dash had felt a long time ago, when he'd allowed himself to sink that deep into creativity. Before he'd become a suspicious bastard by necessity.

It was what he'd allowed to happen today until he remembered that he had to stay on his game.

Lucky lowered the camera. Blinked. Stood silent for several minutes, coming down from the self-imposed high.

"That's fucking cool. Forgot everything for a while," he said, then frowned when he realized the irony of his words.

"I'm glad. It's important to be able to pull away like that," Dash told him.

Lucky nodded, and then he pulled a pack of pictures out of his back pocket. Dash didn't have to look at them to know what they were. "I figured the pictures you had me look through must have something to do with the capture. I knew it at the time, but after you told, me, I looked again."

"How'd you figure it out?"

"It's the only place you've been back to four times." He'd forgotten about the dates on the backs of the photos.

"That mission…what a fuck-up. It was like shit went wrong from before we got in country. Jim kept saying it was a good sign but I couldn't shake the feeling that it wasn't." Dash was aware of Lucky studying the pictures of the road.

"You went back there to take this?"

"I had to."

"Did it help?"

"Not as much as you."

Lucky kissed the side of his neck, breathed against Dash's skin.

"So really, you lost everything you had in order to save me," Dash said. "And you saved me again. And this has nothing to do with the fact that I feel like I owe you. Because you have to know that's not why this happened. It was coincidence, but it wasn't, not after that first night. If I hadn't turned you in…we wouldn't be here."

Lucky turned to him, camera dangling by the strap in his hand. "Those guys who took me—who tried to turn me… whether I get my memory back or not, I'm always going to be their target, right?"

It wasn't anything they'd ever discussed, but of course, he knew. "Yeah, I would've told you, but it's not like you're not dealing with a lot of shit already."

"I can put a lot on my shoulders, Dash. Gotta stop

babying me."

"Is that what I've been doing?"

"Yes. Even when you were suspicious as shit, you were babying me." Dash nodded. "Can't make any promises, but I'll try."

Lucky looked around, conscious of their surroundings. "We need to get to a place where I can kiss you. Now."

Dash agreed.

21

Jace dropped him off at the marina and Sawyer took his sneakers off and padded barefoot to the dock.

Rex was waiting in the boat. When Sawyer jumped in, he noted that Rex had food and beer laid out on deck. Rex nodded in his direction and steered the boat through the slip and out into the open waters.

Sawyer stood next to him as he steered, watching the sun go down, smelling the fresh brine as it battered his cheeks.

He'd trained like a beast today. Had barely taken a break to eat, did so only because he'd needed to keep his body and mind fueled. Jace stayed with him, because that's what best friends did, and even though Jace and Clint were very much together, Sawyer knew he and Jace would always stay best friends.

"You think that bothers Clint?" he asked Rex now.

"I think he knows what you went through together. It's a whole different level of friendship. Clint has a few of them, and so do I."

"Yeah." Somehow, that made Sawyer feel better when

maybe it should make him feel worse.

Maybe if his mother had more in her life, she'd have been able to move on. Maybe she'd made love a crutch and that's what had ruined her for other men.

Because you're not empty, he told himself. Out loud, he muttered, "I'm an idiot."

Rex ran a hand through Sawyer's hair, an affectionate, personal gesture that always made Sawyer hard, and Rex knew it, which is why he did it. Because he'd always look between Sawyer's face and then down to his dick and back up with a small grin on his face.

Pride.

"Maybe we went too fast."

"Or maybe we went just right," Rex told him. "Work's always going to get in the way. We've got to find out how to fit in more fishing trips."

Sawyer smiled. "That'd be cool."

"I'm glad you stuck with me through this, Sawyer. I know it's been shitty."

Tomorrow was Sawyer's twenty-eighth birthday. And even though they both knew that cancer didn't always mark itself off on an exact calendar, the fact that Sawyer had gotten past his grandfather's age of when his cancer had returned was a huge milestone. Something that had weighed so heavily on Sawyer's mind for so damned long. And he never wanted Sawyer to go through anything alone.

"Relationship shit's hard," Sawyer said.

"Guess that's what makes it worth it. If it was easy, everyone would do it right." Rex cut the engine, dropped the anchor and turned the lights on. They were in a cove, farther than they'd been the other night.

He motioned for Sawyer to sit on deck and joined him. He spread blankets out and had a picnic of cold foods, lots of seafood, like lobster rolls and potato salad, and as they ate, they talked about their days. Rex was jealous that Sawyer got to spend it outside and free, because he'd been stuck in meetings all day.

After he'd said that, he'd looked at Sawyer and said, "I fucking hate lying to you."

"You weren't in meetings all day?"

"I was in therapy sessions. Meetings with JAGs. Navy officials."

Sawyer's stomach tightened. "Because of Lucky."

"Yes. And since there are no indications that I knew he was alive, no contacts made, I'm sure things will be fine. But right now, it's hell not being one hundred percent believed. I can only imagine what it's doing to Lucky."

There was always a pause right before Rex used the name Lucky, like he had to try really hard not to let "Josh" slip out.

"But I didn't bring you out here to talk about that. I brought you out here to…well, you shared your past. I've acted like letting you into what happened to me during my time in captivity made everything okay, like you said. And it's mostly because I don't want to deal with it, not because I don't want to share it."

Sawyer pushed his food to the side and lay down on one of the big pillows Rex had put out. Rex joined him and they lay side by side, the boat's easy rocking reassuring. But Sawyer didn't touch him, was afraid that if he did, they'd be having sex in seconds. Not that that would be the worst thing, but when Rex was ready to talk, Sawyer needed to listen.

"You never mention your parents," Sawyer said after Rex had been silent for a while.

"Didn't know them. I was left on the church steps. Brought to an orphanage. I stayed there for several years."

"I thought babies got adopted pretty easily."

"Girls more than boys, but yeah, they typically do. I was too serious, from what they told me later."

Sawyer grabbed for Rex's hand. "You were born that way then."

"I didn't cry or coo or any of that stuff, so everyone through there was something wrong with me. Obviously, I don't remember that, but I was pretty much in group foster- home-type situations until I was twelve. Then a family took me in. They liked it because I didn't cause trouble and they collected a paycheck. And they were nice enough. Disinterested. But I had my own room and food. Roof over my head."

"And you think that was enough?"

"I didn't know any better. And don't feel sorry for me." He smiled when he said it. "I thought life was serious and I like being quiet and serious. Observing. I learn a hell of a lot that way."

"Basically, I drive you crazy because I move around all the time." As he spoke, he realized he'd been jiggling his foot the entire time he'd been lying here.

"Not at all. You're exactly what I need to remind me that I'd be missing out on so many of the good parts of life without you."

"I really owe Lucky."

Rex's brow furrowed.

"Because I'm guessing he's the one who showed you how to love. And then you were able to show me. So I definitely owe him."

Rex smiled. "If you look at it that way, yes. Lucky and I bonded because we came from similar backgrounds. We had each other's backs because of that, and it never stopped. Never will. And I need to know if you're really okay with that."

"I'm really okay with it."

22

Lucky sat in the familiar therapy room, Dash by his side.

Cooper was obviously shaken. Lucky rubbed his palms nervously on his thighs and noted that Cooper looked at him oddly.

"What? Josh wouldn't have shown his nerves?" The added sarcasm didn't help the already tense situation.

"No, he wouldn't have," Cooper answered, cutting a look to Dash.

"Can you just tell me what you brought me here for?" Lucky asked. Because Dash had been weird since he'd ushered Lucky into the car after receiving a phone call from Cooper.

It was two in the morning, not exactly prime time for a therapy session, which meant that Cooper had news. And Lucky might not remember things, but he knew innately that phone calls in the middle of the night could rarely bring good news.

Cooper held up an envelope, plain manila with no writing on it. "I found this in my car tonight. I brought it right back in here and played it."

"No indication who it's from?"

"None. I can send it to forensics, but I thought you'd want to see it first," Cooper told them. He'd put on rubber gloves when he touched the envelope and the CD case and the CD contained within. He put it into the computer and turned the large screen around toward Lucky and Dash. Instinctively, Lucky sat forward, and next to him, Dash mirrored his actions.

The screen started off with a jerk, as though someone wasn't used to holding a video camera. The background was black and then got lighter and Lucky got dizzy just watching.

There were voices in the background. Spanish. English.

Next to him, Dash froze. Lucky didn't have to look at Dash to know, but he felt it instantly. He kept his eyes trained on the screen, not wanting to miss a goddamned thing, because this was important. He knew it in his bones.

After several more minutes of nothing on the screen but dizzying movement, Lucky finally realized the person holding the camera down had been walking. Maybe hadn't even realized the camera was on.

That was made clearer when the user put the camera down, sideways, and Lucky saw himself and two other men on the screen.

Cooper rotated the computer screen so they could watch the video right side up.

Lucky realized that he looked much the way he had in the lie detector video—the long hair, the beard, but he was thinner. Pale. Bloody.

He looked like hell on the screen. Could barely hold his head up. The men spoke to him, rapid-fire Spanish—had he known Spanish at one point? So many therapy sessions, so many points to remember.

Josh had known so many things, had been good at them all.

Lucky couldn't decipher a word. It was like watching a movie for the first time. And even though doctors and Rex, Nate and Uncle had pieced together what had happened to him during his time in captivity, he didn't know how things ended up for him, at least not after he was taken from the others and before he was dumped into the water.

Would he find out here? Or would this be just another frustrating piece in the incomplete puzzle of his life?

"You should turn this off," Dash said through gritted teeth. "He needs to see it," Cooper answered quietly.

"Should've been vetted through me," Dash continued.

Lucky never took his eyes from the screen. Dynamite couldn't have torn him away from it.

There were bruises on his body and face, but no one hit him. Instead, they handed him a cup and he drank out of it. Asked for, and got, more.

In Spanish.

And then the men were talking to him and he was

laughing with them. Nodding in agreement. And then he said something and one of them shook his hand and the other clapped him on the back.

"What did I say?" he asked Dash urgently as the screen froze and the tape ended. "Lucky…"

"Tell me. Fucking tell me what I said." But he knew from the look on Dash's face that was a losing proposition, so he turned to Cooper. "You said you wouldn't lie to me."

Dash stood, like he'd bodily stop Cooper from saying anything, but he didn't move toward the guy.

Cooper finally said, "You told them, 'I'm ready to do anything I need to. Just let them go, like you promised, and I'll do whatever you need.'"

He made Cooper rewind and continue to translate. This time around, Lucky heard "Dashiell" and "Africa" in the mix of the Spanish, and he insisted Cooper tell him every damned thing he said, even though he didn't want to know.

"There's no going back," the disembodied voice on the screen said to Josh, the voice pinging something in Lucky. He couldn't pinpoint it and so he shook it off as merely something that was making him sick, watched himself on the screen, staring at whoever the off-camera man was and telling him, according to Cooper, "I don't want to go back. There's no reason to do so now—I'm where I belong."

Lucky was glad he hadn't gotten out of his seat, not when his world spun and he got dizzy. Dash got on his knees in front of him. Lucky could still see the frozen computer screen over Dash's shoulder, watched his expression of happiness on the screen.

"Listen to me, Lucky. We talked about what a good liar you are. You were probably telling them what they wanted to hear. For survival."

"Rex told me that they used to promise they'd make it all stop, for all of us, if just one of us talked," Lucky said slowly.

"Right. So you might've decided to trick them."

That could be true, but he had no idea if it was or not. "Jesus, Dash," was all he could manage.

"He needs to stay here," Cooper said.

"He's going back with me. He's under my care," Dash responded, never taking his eyes from Lucky's.

Lucky felt shattered, like if he stood, he'd break. But Dash helped him up, walked him out of the room and building and away from the goddamned video. He was vaguely aware of the car ride, hiding in the darkness.

He liked that. When they got inside his apartment he begged Dash not to turn the lights on, and Dash complied.

"Everything okay?" Clint asked. Normally, Rex would bitch at him, ask if he'd ask that every time Rex's number came up.

This time, he said, "No. Is Sawyer there?"

"He's not."

Rex forced himself to remain calm, but the terrible feeling he'd had earlier intensified. "Has Jace spoken to him?"

He heard Clint asking Jace and then he was on speaker with both of them.

"I haven't heard from him since I dropped him at the boat," Jace said.

"We were going to spend the night on the boat, but I got called in. Sawyer dropped me off, said he'd grab some food at the diner and wait for me. I've been calling him and got no answer. I went to the diner. My truck's there, but no sign of Sawyer. The waitresses don't remember him even coming in."

"Rex, what were you called in about?" Clint asked.

"That's just it. When I got there, no one knew anything about me being called in."

23

Lucky curled on his side on the bed. Buried his cheek against the pillow that smelled like Dash and wondered if he was going into some kind of shock. He shivered, even though the room was warm and he was both grateful and worried when Dash pressed his chest against his back, spooning him.

They lay like that, silent, in the dark, for a long time. There was no danger of Lucky sleeping, because his mind was on overdrive.

"Even if I do fall asleep, it won't matter. I'm too fucked up to even have nightmares," he told Dash now.

Dash answered with his face pressed against Lucky's shoulder. Rubbed the scruff of his cheek back and forth until the roughness made Lucky hard.

"Some people dream all the time and never get anywhere close to as good of a time in real life. I'd rather have the real life than the dreams, Lucky."

His voice sounded husky.

"How, Dash? How can you still want me—this—after

seeing that tonight?"

"I'm going to get fucking pissed if you ever ask me that again. Do you understand that?"

"No, I don't understand anything," Lucky shouted back, and damn, that felt good. "Did you hear what I said? I told those guys I'd make sure to get revenge for them. They told me they were taking me to South Africa. I said your goddamned name, Dash." Lucky shook, a head-to-toe tremble he couldn't control. "I would've hurt your family. The only family I've had for the past four years."

"But you didn't. And now, I know you couldn't." Dash didn't seem upset, concentrated on taking Lucky's pants off, and Lucky let him. Wanted Dash's skin on his, wanted to know if Dash was lying.

The man couldn't lie during sex, not now when they'd gotten this close. Lucky'd know, once and for all, if Dash could live with knowing that Lucky might've been turned. That he might've hurt Dash's family.

He was naked on the sheets, the lights still off, when Dash's lubed finger entered him without warning. He gasped, tried to roll onto his belly, but Dash grabbed his hip and held him firmly in place.

Lucky remained on his side. Dash knelt so he could take full advantage of him, used his thigh to spread Lucky's legs and pushed inside. He braced for the burn, waited for the inevitable pleasure he felt he didn't deserve.

Dash would give it to him anyway. Rocked against him

fast, urging him to forget everything except what was happening between them. Showing him that nothing else mattered.

For that moment, nothing else did.

Dash pushed one of Lucky's thighs up so he could gain better traction, sliding his cock in and out of the man easily. Lucky reached up and wound an arm around Dash's neck, trying to gain some leverage.

In response, Dash bent and sucked Lucky's nipple hard, before alternately biting and licking. He also never stopping fucking the man, and Lucky's response was to yell Dash's name, bury his face into the pillow, rubbing it back and forth. He didn't know which end was up, and the look in his eyes was one of dazed lust.

It was the exact place Dash wanted him. Reality sucked for both men now, and if he could bring Lucky to a better place, he'd do it.

He moved out from under Lucky's arm as he began to fuck him in earnest now, the bed rocking, headboard slamming the wall. Lucky didn't know what the hell to do with his body as it jerked helplessly with the rhythm Dash set. He put his free arm over his head, tried to turn further onto his belly, but he couldn't. Not the way Dash held him impaled.

Lucky's hand traveled back to Dash's hip, ran his fingers down to scratch his already too-hot skin as Dash drove into him. He held both of Lucky's wrists to the side.

"Not letting you go, Lucky," he panted.

Lucky shook his head, and whether he was agreeing or not, Dash couldn't tell. And dammit, he didn't want Lucky to have any doubts.

"Not letting you go," he growled now, his voice harsh, his thrusts demanding. "Look at me, dammit."

After a few seconds, Lucky did. The first real eye contact he'd made with Dash since they'd left Cooper's office. Even though it was in the dark, it still made all the difference in the world.

He could find this man in the dark. Didn't matter that Lucky thought he could hide.

Dash could see right through him, always had been able to.

He bent down again and kissed Lucky. Hard and fast, then soft, slow and gentle, like he'd never stop. The kisses were everything, all the promises, all the reassurances Dash could give him.

He couldn't answer why—how—all of this happened. It was the last thing he'd have ever expected. But he and Lucky had been bound from the first moments the SEAL team stepped into the jungle to rescue him. And that bond hadn't been cut. Instead, it tugged them closer, across oceans. Across impossible odds.

"Lucky, I've got to run out for a little while. Got a call from my supervisor. Nothing to do with your case. I'll be back and we'll go to breakfast."

Lucky heard Dash's words through his sleep haze, nodded, felt the warm brush of the man's lips against his cheek. And then the body heat was gone and Lucky drifted back and forth between sleep, but he'd gotten his fill.

His body remembered the Navy, even though his mind didn't. Rex had told him that he'd never slept more than four or five hours a night, and when they went out on missions, sometimes it was four or five hours over the course of days.

He sat up now and looked around the darkened room. It was just past five in the morning. He wondered what the hell was up in Dash's world. Wondered if the man was being pulled into another mission, and, as selfish as it was, wondered what that would mean for the two of them.

His mind went back to the tape. How could it not? Dash had tried his best to erase it with mind-blowing sex and had succeeded for a long while. He'd also succeeded in convincing Lucky that he didn't care what had happened in those jungles.

"You're alive. So am I. That's all that fucking matters. We didn't let those bastards win," he'd whispered to Lucky before Lucky heard him softly snore.

Lucky desperately wanted to believe that he'd been faking it with those men. That he'd let his team believe he was dead because it was the only way he could help them.

But he'd have to let that go, or it would haunt him forever. *There's no reason to go back there now.*

He'd said that on the tape.

He was up out of bed, repeating the words, over and over. It wasn't a memory of the past. Not at all.

It was a memory of Cooper, from one of their therapy sessions. When Dash was there with him. When they were talking about recreating the torture and Cooper refused. Told Lucky, *there's no reason to go back there now.*

Coincidence? Or a trigger?

He rubbed his arms up and down. His body froze, like it was bracing for danger.

Because he wasn't alone in the room anymore. "It wasn't Dash's supervisor who called him," he said into the dark.

Cooper's voice answered him. "No. But he won't be back for a while."

24

Lucky woke with a cough. His head pounded. He didn't remember anything after Cooper telling him that he'd taken care of Dash.

But at least he fucking remembered.

Now, he tried to move and found the ropes tight around him. He was flat on his back, a light shining in the corner. He turned his head and saw a shadow in the corner. "That you, Cooper?"

"Glad you remembered."

"Fuck you. What the hell did you do to Dash?"

"Don't worry—he's fine. You won't be, but he'll live to remember all of this." And then Cooper repeated what Lucky assumed to be the same words. In Spanish. The same distinctive Spanish from the video, and that was what had made Dash start.

It wasn't the Spanish of a native speaker.

"You were…there? You were in the room with me?" he asked as the pieces began to tumble together like a house of cards in reverse.

"Give the SEAL a medal," Cooper said, then spoke what seemed like the same sentence again, this time in perfect Spanish that Lucky remembered from the video. The same goddamned voice. It had jarred him in Cooper's office, but he hadn't known exactly why. He knew now—the man's tone was familiar. Lucky had spoken to him several times a day for months and months now. He'd heard Cooper speak in Spanish before...but it was a hazy memory. He'd swear he'd dreamed it, *if* he dreamed. He frantically fought through the past months, to all the time he'd spent with Cooper. To the times Cooper sedated him.

They'd discussed the fact that sodium pentothal wasn't widely used anymore because it was controversial—many believed the subject would be susceptible to memories that could be planted rather than true memories. But Cooper told Lucky that he'd had good luck with it, and Lucky had been so determined to get his memories back, had trusted Cooper so much that he hadn't paid much attention to the fact that Cooper was basically telling him he'd be vulnerable.

He was paying attention now.

"Yes, *Lucky*, I was there. I put a lot of hard work into you, and I didn't get paid because you didn't follow through."

"So why bother with all of this? You knew you couldn't turn me again."

"I could've, if you'd been taking the medication the way you were supposed to."

Lucky hated those meds. Took a few the day he had to

have his blood tested so the levels would show, and shunned them the rest of the time.

"I've gotten Dash and Rex out of the way. And I've already got Rex's new boyfriend, Sawyer," Cooper continued. "I've been staking him out for weeks."

Lucky stared at the man he'd goddamned trusted.

As if reading his mind, Cooper said, "The old Josh would never have trusted me."

"If I'm not the old Josh, why bother with this?"

"I have my reasons."

Lucky ran through a possible laundry list of them. He couldn't be hypnotized—or could he and Cooper had been plotting suggestions inside his mind this entire time? Same with the sodium pentothal trials Lucky himself had insisted on continuing with.

He forced his panic down. The only way to survive—no, fuck that, he was done merely surviving. The only way to win this was to stay calm and let his operator's instincts take over.

He imagined they would.

Cooper studied him, and Lucky hated that he'd trusted this man with some deep shit. Nothing had been secret, but spilling his fear was something he hadn't minded doing with Dash.

He'd trusted Cooper to get him through this.

"Did you know Dash has been working with me the entire time?" Cooper asked, and then Lucky heard Cooper's voice on tape, then Dash's.

"…There's nothing suspicious. Nothing even remotely so."

"Except that he was dumped near my family, Cooper. How can I ever trust that he wasn't put there to hurt them?"

"I'm sure Dash has told you he trusts you now. Are you sure that's true? I mean, who can you trust, Lucky? You've admitted your instincts were rusty. Guess I'm living proof of that."

Don't react.

And he didn't, not even after hearing another snippet of Dash discussing Lucky as if he was a job. Because he'd known that's what he started out being.

But hearing it out of Dash's mouth while he talked to Cooper stung.

How badly could he have misjudged Dash? He'd spent time fucking the man…

And Dash told you that it usually was all an act for him.

But Lucky refused to buy that. Maybe it started out as that before they'd met, but Dash had been fighting his feelings from the first night. It was in the man's touch. The way Dash had calmed him after Nate had upset him.

The way Dash came here and stayed. Watched him.

And that couldn't have been an act.

Could Dash have been pretending everything?

And this is what Dash has been dealing with since he met me. Unsure of what was truth about Lucky and what was made-up. Unsure of what to believe, or whether or not to believe at all.

Lucky had to believe in Dash, and vice versa. He clung to his belief like his lifeline, because he needed something strong enough to hold on to in order to get through whatever Cooper had planned for him. "Tell me what you want me to do. Let Sawyer go."

"No, but good try."

He flexed his hands automatically, reflexively testing the length and tightness of the cuffs.

Cooper smiled.

He knows more about me than I do.

A sobering thought that led to an even better one. Maybe he could use that knowledge against Cooper.

All of a sudden, the room shifted sharply. That was the first time Lucky realized they were in the lower quarters of a boat, out on the open—and suddenly rough—waters.

"I'll let you two get to know each other," Cooper said. "It'll hurt more that way."

Lucky strained, trying to see. He turned his head to the left and finally saw another outline maybe three feet from him, this time of a long, coffin-like box. Just like Rex and Dash had described to him.

"He's trying to recreate the torture," a voice said.

"Sawyer?"

"Hope you weren't expecting someone else to be captured. I think we're enough." He sounded tired, but lucid.

"Are you okay?"

"What do you think?"

"Fuck." He strained at the ropes and then decided not to waste his energy. Cooper needed a mental game. Lucky had to trust that, between him and Sawyer, they could do that.

"I wanted him to recreate the torture—but on me."

Sawyer snorted a little. "Be careful what you wish for."

"You think he's recording us?"

"I'm sure of it." Sawyer paused. "Do you have the scars?"

He drew in a deep, shaky breath and stared down at his hands. "My back, backs of my thighs, just like Rex and Nate and Uncle. They never healed."

"I think you're all brave as fuck," Sawyer told him.

"I don't remember anything."

"Doesn't take away what you did. You're a hero. Gotta remember that, even with all the shit happening."

The fact that Sawyer was complimenting him, talking to him like they weren't captured, like he wasn't locked in a box, made Lucky truly pull himself together. Because if Sawyer could do it, then Lucky needed to believe that, somewhere deep inside him, he had the same training to pull this off. "Have you been captured before?"

"No. I've been cornered though. My teammate and I waited in a cave—it was fight the tide or the rebels. We chose the easier of the two options. And we almost died." Sawyer sighed. "You'd think you'd only have to go through shit like that once in a lifetime."

"I'm sorry I didn't meet you before this."

"I wanted to. But Rex was worried. Rightly so, it looks like."

"And who'd have thought it was the goddamned shrink? That's so fucked up. More fucked up that I didn't think to be suspicious of him," Lucky said angrily.

He saw the box shift a little, was pretty sure Sawyer was trying to work his way out. Lucky was doing the same to the ropes, trying to budge the knots until his fingers ached. But he wouldn't stop.

They would keep talking, to distract Cooper. And each other. Like a final confession they both hoped to hell wouldn't be final.

"Rex still thinks of you as family—he wasn't lying when he told you that," Sawyer continued. "And I'm cool with that. But man, I keep thinking, if none of this had happened to you, if you had your memory, you'd be with Rex. And it's like, fuck, that's not fair. You lost everything trying to save someone. Shouldn't lose the man you love too."

"Ah, Sawyer, no one can go back and predict what would've happened. Maybe Rex and I would've stayed together. Maybe we would've had too much fucked-up guilt between us to do that. And maybe we'd have fallen apart, no matter what. But it did happen. What matters now is how you and Rex feel about each other."

"And suppose you woke up tomorrow with a memory?

Your last memory of Rex would be…"

"That I loved him? I don't see how I can wake up with a memory and feel the way I did four years ago. Too much has happened…and it's not like I'd lose these past four years of memories…or of Dash. You can't worry about me with this. And you can't let Rex wade in guilt over it. That's bullshit."

Sawyer laughed then. Lucky didn't think he'd said anything particularly funny but hell, maybe if he'd been locked in a box for hours at a time, he'd be laughing inappropriately too.

Sawyer sobered and said, "The guilt's been cutting Rex apart."

Lucky went to respond, but the boat jerked a little. He fell back, his hand landing on something that felt like a lick of fire. He bit his lip to keep from crying out, felt the blood on his hands…and then rooted for the object that cut him.

It was a single, thin razor blade. It hadn't been there moments before.

"The guilt's been cutting Rex apart."

Somehow Sawyer had gotten it to him. How Sawyer got it was another story—but Lucky had spent enough time discussing SEALs with Cooper to know that special forces operators were sneaky, resourceful fucks who never took anything for granted, including their personal safety. For every weapon you saw, there were twenty in hiding.

Cooper had to have patted him down. And he'd be really

pissed that he'd missed it. That thought almost made Lucky smile, but he didn't, because of the cameras.

Instead, he kept his movements small, even as he was cutting his fingers fucking bloody—he felt it, but he went at the ropes as Sawyer talked as cover.

"You know, when Jace and I were waiting for the water to either kill us or let us go, we made promises. We spent what might be the last moments of our lives talking about the guys we loved. I guess that's where everyone goes when they think they're in their final moments—to the people they love."

"Yeah," Lucky said. "Cuts it wide open."

"Yeah," Sawyer echoed, with a smile in his voice. "Your life's wide open. That's kind of cool if you think about it. How many people get a true second chance like that?"

"Not many, I'm guessing."

"Then take it."

"Cooper got a CD that showed Lucky agreeing to help Allen Gonzalves's men. And we watched it together. Lucky was upset. I got a call in the middle of the night from my supervisor. But when I got into the building, I heard Lucky's voice telling me, 'You shouldn't have believed me.' And then I woke up on the floor."

Dash held the ice to his head as he paced around in front

of Rex and Clint and Jace.

"I don't care if he's Lucky or Josh. He wouldn't do this," Rex said firmly.

"Then who?" Clint asked.

"Cooper said he found the CD in his car. He said he had the guards looking at the videotapes of the lot from that time but…"

Clint was on the phone. "I'll check on that."

"Do you have the CD?" Jace asked.

"I grabbed it from Cooper's office," Dash said. He handed it to the younger SEAL, who popped it into a computer, put his headphones on and began to watch.

Dash turned away, not wanting to see it again.

Rex said, "Can you get in touch with Cooper?"

"I called him. Figured he crashed—we left his office at three in the morning." Dash dialed him again. "Do you think he's in danger?"

"Allen might think that Cooper knows anything and everything Lucky told him," Rex pointed out.

Jace held his hand up to silence them. He pulled the headphones off and said, "I pulled some talking out of the background. English and Spanish."

"How'd you do that?" Clint asked.

"My cousin and I used to bootleg records so he could sell them," Jace said casually. "Don't judge. Comes in handy during times like this, right?"

"Just play it," Clint said, and Jace did. There was

English—mumbled and then clear Spanish, although not from a native speaker.

"'He's ready to do anything we need—that's what he said,' was the Spanish," Jace said. "And this English is clearer. 'Make sure not to bring him back to his cell.'"

Dash's head swam. "Play that again—the English."

The room was silent as Jace did so again.

Dash pulled another tape out of his pocket—the kind that would go into a handheld recorder. "Can you match a voice?"

"Yes." Jace pulled up some software as Clint stared at him. "I feel you judging me. I know more than demolitions."

"I think he deserves a promotion," Rex said. "You and Sawyer both."

Jace turned to Rex for a second. "He's too strong to go down, Rex. We'll find him."

And then he loaded the CD into the software. He played it—Cooper and Lucky were talking. Lucky's voice was a perfect match.

So was Cooper's.

"Holy fuck," Rex breathed.

"I know where he lives," Dash said.

The four men were in the truck, with Clint driving. They decided their plan of attack and made the mutual decision not to call for back-up.

"There's no way he brought them here," Jace said quietly.

"But maybe we'll find a way to track him," Clint said,

put a hand over Jace's. As Dash watched from the backseat, his throat tightened. He glanced over at Rex, who was watching the hand holding too.

"We'll find them, Dash. We have to," Rex said.

Dash looked straight ahead until they were in the parking lot of Cooper's building. Clint went up first—out of all of them, he'd be the least known by Cooper. The others waited outside the door as backup.

"He's not here," Clint called after several tense minutes of silence. The other men tore in, careful not to overturn anything that could trigger a bomb.

But the apartment was clean—Jace swept it and declared there were no explosives or bugs. That's when they searched in earnest. There was no computer. No paper trail.

But there were two DVDs left right by the phone. Jace raced them down to the truck to play them, Dash right behind him. Clint and Rex remained to raid the apartment.

Jace loaded the first DVD and angled the laptop's screen so they could both see it. Cooper. Lucky.

Lucky had an IV running into his arm.

"Probably the sodium pentothal," Dash murmured.

He was asking Lucky standard questions about his missing memories. Lucky knew nothing. And then...and then Cooper began to talk in Spanish.

"He's trying to plant memories—new memories," Dash breathed. "Attempting to. Doesn't look like it worked," Jace pointed out. "Unless Cooper's got to hypnotize him to bring it out," Dash said. "Why leave this for us to find?" Jace asked.

"Because he's not coming back," Dash said.

"So this all failed. Lucky doesn't remember anything that could indict Cooper at all," Jace started.

"Maybe he had to make sure? If he remembers anything, he could blow Cooper's entire operation."

"What was his operation?" Jace asked as Clint climbed back into the truck with Rex. "Turning prisoners of war into soldiers for terrorists like Allen Gonzalves?"

"Only for Gonzalves," Clint said grimly, handing a tape to Dash. "We played one in the apartment. Gonzalves is in them, talking to his American-born *brother* named Cooper."

"Fuck me," Dash muttered. "Cooper left that out for me to find."

"They weren't exactly hidden well, so yes," Clint agreed.

"So wait, Gonzalves went missing right after we were released," Rex said.

"Maybe he's not missing," Jace said. "What if Cooper killed him?"

"What if Cooper wants to prove to his brother that he's still worthy of working with him?" Dash said grimly. The men were silent, because neither theory meant anything good for Lucky and Sawyer.

Cooper came back down to the darkened room about half an hour after Lucky had freed his hands. The boat was still rocking, the wind was howling and Sawyer called out, "Dude, you can't leave the boat on auto-pilot in this kind of weather. Jesus is not here to take the wheel."

Lucky bit his lip to keep from laughing. When Cooper calmly began to waterboard Sawyer, he bit his lip to keep from cursing the man.

It was too soon to give away the fact that he was free. Mainly because Cooper had a weapon at his side, and because, with the light from upstairs, Lucky could plainly see that the box with Sawyer inside was wired. That could be a ruse or the real thing, but either way, Cooper must have a bomb planted on board and a trigger somewhere— in his pocket...around his neck. But Lucky couldn't move without risking Sawyer's life.

Maybe you're the fucking trigger.

Christ, that thought made him sweat. He hadn't moved much at all when he was cutting the ropes, but if he had...

"I know how to pilot a boat through storms," Cooper said. "How'd you learn? Your brother?" Sawyer asked.

Brother?

"Did you know that, Lucky? The guy who nearly killed you and Rex and Dash—he was Cooper's brother. Cooper couldn't resist bragging about that shit."

The waterboarding happened again. Lucky screwed his eyes shut, like that could helpSawyer.

Sawyer, who coughed and said, "I was trained for this, you dumbshit."

"Is it true?" Lucky asked Cooper.

"Yes, it is. I am Allen's half brother. I was brought up in the States. I've been working with him for years, helping him torture and turn American soldiers—"

"We're sailors," Sawyer pointed out.

He's really good for Rex.

It was an oddly inappropriate thought. But one Sawyer would no doubt appreciate.

"So isn't it better that Lucky has no memories of you?" Sawyer continued to Cooper. "I mean, he doesn't fucking remember you. Cut your losses."

"I'm getting tired of you."

"Ditto."

More water. More coughing. This time, Sawyer stayed silent, but Lucky let his instincts guide him. Sawyer was giving him the opening this time. Because there was something Josh might know that Cooper needed him to remember. But what? What the hell would Josh have known that Cooper didn't?

"What are you doing, Cooper? What the fuck do you need from me?" he asked.

"I'm going to let you watch me break Sawyer, since you wanted to see torture so badly. Since you can't remember and appreciate my hard work, I'll bring you and Sawyer to Allen and I'll let you watch every painful minute of Sawyer's torture. And then I'll make sure you don't survive the water."

"Was I meant to the first time?" he demanded.

"You were supposed to murder Dash's family, like we primed you to do. They walked on the beach every single night. You were going to kill them. Cut their heads off and send them to Dashiell as a message that no one escapes our family. And then you lost your goddamned memory."

"Did you hit me during the fucking torture? Because then you're the reason why all my memories are missing, you asshole. You fucked yourself over."

Sawyer laughed. The man was tied up in a box, with water being poured inside the small hole he breathed out of repeatedly and he was laughing. "Fuck. I really fucking like you."

Cooper poured the water in to shut him up. Lucky heard the silence, the sputter, then the coughing.

And then the laughing.

Yeah, he really fucking liked Sawyer too.

"Cooper had a boat," Jace said. "I just ran it through motor vehicles. It's parked at the Marina with Rex's."

Clint cursed as they drove to the marina, muttered

something about never wanting to be a squid in the first place, and Jace dragged him on the boat.

The weather had turned, violently so.

"I'll give you a life preserver," Jace told him as Rex piloted the boat through the waters. It was dark and stormy, which had them rethinking their decision not to call for help. The Coast Guard was already searching for the boat by air and sea. They'd also warned Rex not to go out, but they knew he wasn't going to listen.

"He couldn't have gotten far in this," Rex said. "Neither will we," Clint pointed out.

"We will if we follow them." Jace motioned to the helo overhead that dragged a light through the water ahead of them. "That's Glen. He knows we're here. He's going to help guide us while he looks."

Lucky heard the chopper before Cooper did. Sawyer started to sing louder, probably to cover that up too. Needed them to get closer as the boat rocked in the choppy water and Cooper kept cutting him.

Lucky could only see the knife going up and down, a sharp glint in the dark. And through it all, Sawyer kept singing. Dirty sailor limericks.

"Soon, you won't be laughing. You have no idea how many men I've turned," Cooper said.

"How many?" Sawyer asked. "I'm genuinely curious about what number you'll think I'll be. Because I'm thinking you thought Lucky was turned too. Maybe he never was. Is that why you're so pissed now?"

At Sawyer's words, Lucky was up, brandishing the razor. He moved forward, clicking open the outside lock on the box Sawyer was held in. And then he knocked the gun from Cooper's hand and had him on the floor, the razor over the man's carotid.

"One strong rock of the boat and you're gone," he warned.

"You took a chance. How did you know you weren't the trigger?" Cooper asked with a sick-looking smile that twisted Lucky's gut.

"He was the trigger." Sawyer was climbing out of the box as a sudden, small explosion from the bilge toward the back of the boat made it shake and then list. It wouldn't take much to punch a hole in the bilge, which would cause the boat to sink at a rapid pace. "And now we're fucking sinking, so let's get on deck."

"You are fucking coming with us," Lucky told Cooper, who lunged up so the razor cut him deep. Blood spurted everywhere as Lucky ripped off his T-shirt and tried to staunch the flow. "Fucker."

Sawyer was running upstairs, no doubt going to signal for help and try to steer the rapidly listing boat. Lucky pressed his shirt to Cooper's neck. Then he tied the guy's hands and dragged him up onto the deck that already had water up to mid-calf.

The front of the boat was billowing smoke, and already half submerged.

"You couldn't have thought you'd survive this," Lucky said. But from the look in the man's eyes, it was apparent he had.

"Lucky, come on—they're sending down a basket," Sawyer shouted. "You go—you're hurt."

"No way—put the asshole on it. Let's let him live so I can kill him."

As the helo hovered overhead, bright lights flashed across the deck.

"Tell me that's someone for us," he called.

"It's Rex's boat," Sawyer yelled back.

They'd be saved, but Cooper was obviously dying. "And I still don't have my fucking memories," he yelled to him.

"If this didn't…do it," Cooper gurgled and Lucky had to put his ear so close to the dying man to hear him. "Never… happening."

"Cooper, come on, just fucking tell me…was I lying? Or was I really brainwashed?" Lucky yelled over the wind again into Cooper's face.

Cooper stared up at him. As he spoke, Lucky leaned

in once more to hear his last words. "You were…so good, man. I wasn't…ever able…to tell…the difference."

When Lucky pulled away, Cooper's eyes held that blank stare of the dead. And then the boat shifted violently. He was slammed away from Cooper's body, nearly went overboard. He managed to hang onto the deck with one arm, yanked himself up as the waves threatened to pull him under.

"Not letting you go that easily."

It was Rex. Holding on to him. Pulling him back onto Cooper's boat, then helping him across the sinking deck and onto the boat where they'd already pulled Sawyer. He took Dash's arm and heaved himself over onto the safe boat. Rex jumped in behind him, hugged him hard. And then they all went to Sawyer.

Jace grabbed Sawyer. "Are you okay?"

"I just want to get out of the fucking water!" he yelled. Jace pulled Sawyer tight against him.

"We'll be fine if we move. Glen will spot us," Rex said as the boat listed along with the waves. "Sawyer, you hang on."

"Tell him I'm fine," Sawyer said to Jace, gritted his teeth as Jace pressed the bandages hard to his wounds as Clint held them both steady.

Lucky helped hold the lights, along with Dash. All of them were soaked. Most of them were in shock. But they were all alive.

25

"Never. Leaving. You alone. Again." Dash's words were punctuated by his thrusts. Lucky lay under him, and for the past half an hour and for the past two days, his only basic choice had been to agree with whatever Dash said.

"Yeah, Dash," he said now.

"You might think you're humoring me. But I'm fucking serious."

"Yes, Dash."

Dash pinned him, hands overhead, his thigh splitting Lucky's legs open. Cock against cock. Kissed the hell out of him, until Lucky moaned into his mouth.

"Want to take you away with me, baby."

"On a job?"

"Photography."

"And that's code for…"

"Photography."

Lucky shivered as Dash's fingers brushed his gland. "I'm in."

"That would be me."

Lucky rolled his eyes. "I meant the trip."

"We'll be gone for months."

"Good. And you'll teach me what you know about taking pictures."

"And more."

Sawyer watched Rex from the hospital bed. The man was fucking fluttering. Fluffing pillows. Pouring water. Talking to doctors and nurses. Checking on Sawyer without actually talking to him.

When he asked the nurse about the bedpan, Sawyer lost it. Pushed the tray away and forced himself to sit up, despite the screaming pain that had set in.

Some of the wounds were deeper than others. Some would scar, some wouldn't. Rex got a plastic surgeon in so that would minimize any issues.

There was one up the side of his neck and one under his chin—Cooper had been waiting to cut his face up last. At least that's what he'd told Sawyer.

"That's enough," Sawyer said calmly.

"That's not enough. Lie back down and heal." Rex paused, like he knew how ridiculous that sounded.

But Sawyer was up and in his face. "Can you look at me, Rex? Can you fucking look at me?"

Rex was having trouble with that. Sawyer, not so gently,

took Rex's chin in his hand and forced him to. "I'm okay."

"I know that. I was there."

"No, you weren't. And that's okay that you weren't."

Rex's nostrils flared. He ground his teeth together. Finally managed, "No, it's not," before he jerked out of Sawyer's grasp.

"Sawyer."

"God, no," he muttered at the sound of his mother's voice. He stood in the hospital gown with his ass hanging out and watched her come in—and she wasn't even fluttering as much as Rex—before she hugged him.

Or tried to. He held back and it took her a moment to realize why. "Oh, honey, I'm sorry. You're out of bed so I thought…"

"He's a strong guy," Rex said.

Sawyer's mom turned to look at him. "Oh, hello. I'm Jude Kirke, Sawyer's mother."

"Mom, this is my CO," Sawyer said and Rex shook her hand and said, "I'll leave you two alone."

But Sawyer wasn't done talking. "And he's also Rex, the man I'm in love with."

She looked between the men. "But you brought Jace to the party. Are you broken up with him?"

Sawyer's mouth hung open and then Rex began to laugh. And laugh. And he didn't stop until Sawyer joined him.

"I'll just give you two a moment," Sawyer's mom said as Sawyer moved toward Rex. He leaned into the man's chest with his shoulder and Rex buried his nose in Sawyer'shair.

"I fucking thought I lost you."

"But you didn't."

"I'm sorry, Sawyer. I've been here for you."

"I know. But now you're really here. And I'm all right. I'm tougher than you think."

"You're not that tough, which is good. I don't want you to pretend. If there's fallout from this…"

"What? You'll put up with my nightmares?" Sawyer asked, half joking.

"Hell yeah." Rex gave a small smile. "I love you, Sawyer. Sometimes, it feels like too much, but I know there's no suchthing."

"Love you, Rex. Really fucking love you."

"When you love someone, you tend to listen to them."

"When you love someone, you don't mention the word *bedpan*."

Rex snorted and Sawyer started laughing again, even though it hurt, and they stayed that way until Sawyer's mom came back in, trailed by his nurse, who yelled at them both.

Rex watched the video, hunched forward, his hands fisted on his thighs. He looked so tense, like he could snap in half. Nate stood behind him and Uncle refused to watchit.

He was waiting in the other room.

Sawyer stood next to Dash, unable to look away from the man on the screen.

And Lucky stood at the window, unwilling to watch the damned thing again. It played in his mind, a continuous loop, and he wondered if he'd ever rid himself of it.

He hadn't wanted Dash to show this to anyone, never mind the men who were actually now watching it. But after what had happened with Cooper, finding out that he'd been the one who'd really been the traitor, Dash had felt Rex, Nate and Uncle had a right to know everything.

The Navy obviously agreed. They were granting Lucky a discharge, with several conditions that Dash promised to help fulfill, the least of which were continued therapy visits. With a therapist of Lucky's choosing this time.

And, based on the intel they'd gotten from Cooper's files, the Navy had sent in a team to infiltrate Gonzalves's secret compound. They'd done so, figuring that once Gonzalves discovered his half brother had been killed, he would be looking to retaliate.

According to the SEAL team that took him down, his plans were in motion to do just that.

Lucky guessed that Cooper had decided that if he went down, he was taking his half brother with him. Jace was pissed that his team wasn't allowed in, but after all that had happened with Rex, there was no way they'd have been assigned that.

The video had ended. The room was so goddamned silent. Lucky put his forehead against the cold window, closed his eyes until he heard Rex say, "Lucky," in a hoarse voice.

Fuck, he didn't want to answer, didn't want to know what he thought of him.

Rex knew him better than probably anyone else in the world at one point in time.

Lucky knew that Dash was hoping Rex could give them some closure on this.

Lucky wasn't sure he believed that one man could be granted that many miracles in a lifetime, but he felt he had surely been.

"Lucky, look at me."

Rex, again. Lucky didn't turn around, or maybe he couldn't. It didn't matter anymore.

When Rex came close to him, Lucky whispered, "Just say it, Rex. I can take it. Just fucking tell me what you're thinking."

"You were lying on the video."

He turned around like a shot to face Rex. "How do you know? You can't know that for sure."

"Yeah, he can," Nate said after he cleared his throat. "We had…contingencies for shit like that."

"What are you talking about?" Dash asked, and Uncle came through the door, asking, "Did he make the sign?"

"Yeah, he did," Rex said, without taking his eyes from

Lucky. "The sign?" Lucky echoed.

"Yeah. Like a safe word only we know—you're in trouble and you've got to pretend to go along with them. It's something to let us know that you were just fucking with the enemy," Uncle said. He rewound the tape and pointed to the cup of water Josh had handed back to the men and then to Josh's fingers on his other hand, the way he touched his middle fingertip to his pointer nail, a fast, subtle movement that Lucky wouldn't have noticed. No one would've...

Unless you were looking for it.

Rex reached out and grabbed him in a tight embrace. "You were lying, Lucky. You were never turned. And I hope to God you never remember the shit you went through to pull that off. That's a fucking blessing, a miracle. Don't ask why. Just goddamned accept it."

26

Four months later

"I'm so goddamned sore," Lucky groaned. He shoved his board into the sand and stared back out at the waves. Uncle came up beside him.

"You're not seriously complaining about rough surf to me, are you?" Uncle asked. Lucky had seen the surgical scars mixed in with the scars from his captivity, knew that the doctors had told Uncle he'd never be able to bear weight on his badly healed arms and they'd forced him into retirement.

Uncle had shown them. Although he wasn't as strong as he'd been—according to Nate—he outsurfed them all. He was the one grabbing them up from out of the waves every time they wiped out.

It was a role well suited to the sandy-haired man who always seemed relaxed. But Lucky knew better—behind that vibe, Uncle was always on patrol.

"Did you teach me to surf?" Lucky asked now, because he'd just realized it. Emme had gotten him on the board years ago and he'd taken to it quickly. Too quickly.

"You were a natural. You caught on quick and you were damned good. " He paused. "Rex hates to surf. Can't get the hang of it. Falls every time."

"That is false information," Rex called. "Sheesh, what if I wasn't here to defend my reputation?"

"I have video proof of your surfing suckiness," Uncle told him seriously.

Lucky looked at Rex and Sawyer—Rex had an easy arm slung over Sawyer's shoulder. Sawyer's scars were well healed. Some had even faded so much they probably wouldn't be visible within the next few months.

But they all had them, visible or not.

"Hey." Dash wrapped his arms around Lucky's waist and stared over his shoulder. "I hope you vetted that new guy Emme's hanging out with."

"He seems all right, big brother." Lucky looked over to where Emme and Jack played in the water.

"Her bikini's too small," Dash said.

"Anyone ever tell you that you're way too overprotective?"

"You. All the time. You know what I say?"

"What?"

"Get used to it."

Lucky would. The road back would never be easy, but now that none of them were looking over their shoulders, Lucky's past didn't seem to matter as much. Not when he had his future in front of him.

NEWSLETTER

Sign up for the newsletter of SE Jakes and her alter-ego Stephanie Tyler!

Be among the first to learn not only about new and upcoming books but also appearances and signings as well as special promotions and giveaways!

http://stephanietyler.com/newsletter/

NOW AVAILABLE:

HOLD THE LINE

AN *INKED* NOVELLA

TURN THE PAGE
TO READ AN EXCERPT...

HOLD
THE LINE

INKED 1

*Holding on loosely has never
been such a challenge...*

What happens when a tattoo artist and a Delta Force soldier keep a promise and take a cross-country trip together? Quinn and Con are about to finally meet and find out. Quinn thinks he's the responsible one, but he quickly learns that he needs to loosen up if he's got any shot of holding onto Con.

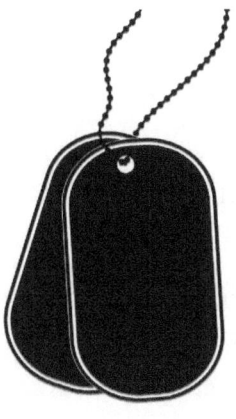

CHAPTER 1

Quinn McKenna glanced down at the stack of paper that had arrived certified mail just hours before, care of his younger brother, and then back up at the man hanging out by the pool table.

He didn't have a picture of Conlan "Con" Jenkins in his packet—just a basic description—but he realized now he'd have known the tall, handsome Delta Force soldier anywhere. There was something in his bearing that Quinn picked out easily. Maybe it was because Quinn's father and brothers had been Delta too, so he was in tune with the way they operated. Most of the Special Forces soldiers he'd come in contact with in his younger days, including his father and his brothers, appeared so outwardly casual to the rest of the world, blending in when they needed to. But Quinn knew that Con was consistently on alert, and that, if asked, he'd be able to give a description of every single person in the place tonight.

Bet you'll find him playing pool, Scott had also offered next to the name of the bar/restaurant picked for the initial meet-up, then added, *He'll be the one winning, with a lot of pissed-off guys around him.*

So yes, Quinn'd picked Con almost from the start, but remained at his table, casually scoping the soldier out while he ate dinner. He noted both he and Con were early for their meet-up, and wondered if they'd both been trying to outmaneuver the other. Not that there was any reason for that kind of thing—this was supposed to be a fun trip, not a competition. A trip ordered by Scott, and something neither Quinn nor Con could—or would—refuse.

Quinn could hear that phone conversation echoing in his ears.

"Bring my best friend to me," Scott had ordered him three weeks ago on the phone, and in Con's paperwork, Quinn now saw that Scott had written, *Bring my brother home to me.*

When they'd spoken on the phone weeks earlier, Scott had also explained, "Con's dangerous with too much time on his hands."

Quinn remembered wanting to bang his head against the wall but had asked instead, "How dangerous?"

"You'll travel with him for a couple of weeks—you tell me."

Quinn immediately understood just what his brother

meant, because Con was obviously well versed at hustling pool. The guys he'd been playing had gone from friendly to very disgruntled, and Con either noticed and didn't give a shit or else he was oblivious.

Quinn was betting on the former.

Then again, Con had refused the bets at least six times, had told the men asking that it wouldn't be fair, and not in a cocky, assholeish way. But the men weren't listening and Quinn knew there was a fight in Con's future. And that meant there'd be a fight in Quinn's as well.

There was still time to bail. He glanced at his watch, noting he was still early enough that Con wouldn't miss him if he left. Unless Con had pegged him from the moment he'd walked in.

Scott wants this, he reminded himself. And he wouldn't refuse his brother, no matter how badly he wanted to.

And he really wanted to. But Scott couldn't make this trip this year, not like he'd planned, and so he'd asked Quinn and Con to do it in his stead. They'd start here, outside of L.A. and end up in the Catskills, and ultimately, Scott's wedding, by way of the strange and varied path Scott had created for them.

By rights, Scott should've been here, a buffer between them, the glue that would bond them. Con and Scott had served together. Sat on the bus together to Basic, and from that point forward they'd been inseparable. Con did come home with Scott for some holidays, but Quinn hadn't been there for any of those. He was the older brother, off sowing his wild oats, which was true. But during that time, he'd also become a licensed tattoo artist. He'd also been featured on a few of those ink shows on reality TV, but he had no real aspirations to be a regular, even though his boss wanted him to be. Mainly because the producers also wanted to include more about his personal life, thinking that would make for great TV.

But this wasn't TV—this was his motherfucking life, as he'd pointed out. His private life was private for a reason, although he'd never made any bones about his sexual orientation, or his bent toward BDSM. The writers of the show offered to find him love, especially if they could follow him into the club scene.

His boss at the tattoo shop told him he'd cave sooner than later. Right before he'd given Quinn the time off to make this road trip. And if that was a bribe, it was a pretty effective one. So he'd pushed back appointments. But really, Scott did the rest of the work, from the big things like booking hotels and restaurants to the mundane of actually planning the route ("*Con will tend to ramble and he doesn't like to use maps—says he doesn't need them*")—and yeah, that was so *not* how Quinn operated.

But hell, he couldn't deny how handsome Con was. Not pretty boy, no. He was rugged looking, lanky with a swagger that probably made most guys want to be him or fall to their knees and beg to be fucked by him.

It made Quinn want to push Con to his knees and force his cock in between those full lips, watch them swell from sucking as his eyes glazed with pleasure.

You're supposed to be keeping an eye on him, not fucking him.

Did Scott even know if Con was gay, or bi? Did it matter?

What mattered was that this would be the longest trip of Quinn's life.

As soon as Con saw the pool table, he'd known he was fucked. Because he was nervous. Jumpy. And as much as playing pool always got him in shitloads of trouble, it also calmed him.

He'd come back to California forty-eight hours earlier after eight months OUTCONUS. He'd routed through his home post for seventy-two hours and then he'd literally come straight to this bar in Normalsville, USA.

He wasn't ready in any way, shape or form to be around civilians. Scott knew that—it was probably why he'd given Con a chaperone, in the form of Quinn McKenna.

Quinn'd arrived ten minutes after Con. Situational awareness was his job, and a guy like Quinn caught his attention easily. He'd seen pictures, but none had done Quinn justice. He'd walked in like he owned the place.

And he's bossy as fuck, Scott had told him often. And the way Quinn'd marched in, like he was planning on taking and conquering, made Con smile. Mainly because he didn't play by bossy rules. But looking at Quinn…maybe he should start.

Still, Con had been ignoring him for the better part of an hour, in favor of racking up. The pool cue, the chalk, the sharp snick of the balls as they snapped smartly together all drew him in, especially because of the way they mixed with the smell of beer and tobacco and cologne, all the bar chatter and music. The familiar sounds of his childhood.

And the people…he could group them easily, had been born and bred to group them in the most advantageous way possible. The monied set. The good ole boys. The cowards. The troublemakers.

Where Quinn fit in, Con had some idea, but he was open to really finding out. After a few games. And so he'd shot several, fucking up the first break the way he always did. His dad thought that Con had just perfected the art of the scam easily. Con had let him think it.

What was the alternative? *No, Dad. I really didn't fuck up my games on purpose—I let my nerves get the best of me…*

"You had a clear shot. Blind man could've made it."

Con didn't bother glancing up at the sound of the voice. Guaranteed, it was a plaid-shirted guy who'd been sitting at four o'clock, trying to pin him down for a so-called friendly game of pool.

Right now, Con screamed "easy betting money." But Con didn't want to bet on pool, hadn't planned on hustling tonight. The pressure had started from Plaid Shirt and then a few of his friends, and Con suggested they keep it friendly, play for beers. But the guys thought he was chicken. Goaded him.

Finally, because he needed to play pool and make them shut the fuck up, he took the bet. He figured he'd given them enough of an out that he didn't have to feel guilty. Now, an hour later, he was up two grand and up against three pissed-off regulars who would no doubt try to roll him in the parking lot when he left. At this point, they were in the "refusing to let him leave" stage of bargaining. The "just one more game" bullshit, like they'd suddenly get lucky.

Ain't happenin', boys.

Finally, Quinn'd sidled up to the table, looking like just another guy checking out the action. But he wasn't just another guy—he was big and tall and handsome…and he turned a lot of heads. He could probably fight well. But really, Con wouldn't have any problem taking on these guys the way he took their money. He'd told them not to—he'd been truthful, so that absolved him of any guilt he might've had.

Hell, he had enough guilt already—needed a fucking U-Haul for it—and wasn't looking to add more weight to pull.

Instead, he took a drink of the seltzer water that'd been fueling him most of the night and finally made eye contact with Quinn. The two of them were standing slightly away from the pool table, watching Plaid Shirt rack up—again—with the others watching him like they were afraid he'd just disappear into thin air.

Con could definitely do that, but it was more smoke and mirrors than anything. All of this was. So he stared at the big man who looked at him, disapproval written all over his face. It was literally going to be like being watched by Big Brother. Although he looked nothing like Scott, Scott had shared family pictures ad nauseam.

Con had none. In return for warm fuzzy family pictures and their accompanying stories (that Con had actually liked but would never come right out and admit to), Con taught Scott to hustle pool. Well, to assist. Hustling was a skill best learned young and used regularly, especially when someone was depending on it for survival. He'd learned early on that if he didn't hustle, he didn't eat. That's how he'd grown up.

"You're good," Quinn said in a low, deep voice.

"I know," he said irritably as Quinn's dark eyes locked him in place. He swallowed, forced himself to look away.

"How long are you going to keep this up?"

"I've been trying to get out of here for an hour."

"So go."

"Gotta give them a chance to make their money back.

Wouldn't be fair otherwise," Con pointed out.

"Since when's what you do fair?"

Con smirked. "Since now. And you have no idea what I do."

"Hustler with a conscience. Interesting."

Yeah, it was interesting all right. "I'll meet you two exits down the highway."

Quinn raised a brow but didn't say anything.

Con wanted to be annoyed, but he was too busy noticing the tattoos that snaked out from under Quinn's pushed-up shirtsleeves, and one that twined elegantly along the side of Quinn's neck. "Seriously. Don't wait here for me. I'll be fine. Trust me."

Quinn looked between Con and the pool table and gave a soft snort in retort.

Quinn didn't listen to Con's orders, mainly because he didn't take them, not that he didn't believe Con could handle himself. When Con readied to leave, Quinn saw three of the men follow him out. Quinn brought up the rear, walked out onto the dark sidewalk in time to see Con smoothly dispatching the three men, doing barely any damage, but enough to make the men go back inside the bar.

For reinforcements, Quinn figured.

"Ready?" Con called as he got on his Harley, which was parked two spaces over from Quinn's big truck.

"Do we have a choice?" Quinn asked as he started his truck.

Con laughed, a sound that carried over the roar of his own bike. "Unless you want to deal with more of them. I'm happy to do it."

Fuck. Not especially. Was it going to be like this for the entire trip, getting Con's ass out of scrapes?

"You weren't supposed to wait," Con called to him, right before he pulled out into the road. Quinn followed close behind, the two vehicles taking off smoothly into the night and disappearing without anyone following them.

They'd gotten lucky. Quinn knew that. He could only imagine the amount of times a trail of cars had followed Con.

Finally, he pulled off the exit, behind Con, as planned. They parked along the side of the rest stop where they'd have a good view if anyone drove in. It was mainly truckers stopping here this time of night anyway.

Con got off the bike and strolled up to Quinn's truck. Quinn opened the door and slid down to meet him. "What would you do if I wasn't here?"

Con laughed, sounding slightly crazy "What? You think I need you to bodyguard me? Newsflash—I don't."

"Fine. So we ride together and go our separate ways at

night. You can hustle pool and defend your own honor."

"While you rest your old man bones? Sounds good."

"Let's leave my bone out of it," Quinn growled. Con looked right between his legs, letting his gaze linger, then slowly let it drift up to Quinn's face.

God, this fucker needed to be taught a lesson and Quinn was itching to do that, wanted to take him over his lap and…

Con grinned, like he knew what Quinn was thinking. Which wasn't possible. He was military, not psychic.

"We're not doing that every night," Quinn informed him.

"Last I looked, this wasn't a military base and you aren't in charge of me," Con told him.

Quinn raised a brow. "You're looking for someone to take charge?"

Con hesitated for only the briefest second. "Did I say that?"

Well, he might as well have, because dammit, Con was screaming for someone—the right someone—to hold him down and fuck him.

But he was supposed to simply be taking a road trip to see Scott. With Con. "Escorting him," was how Scott termed it. As he put it, "Without you, Con would eventually make it here, probably with a police car in tow."

Quinn glanced at Con. "Doesn't the military have rules?"

"Lots of them. Be specific."

"Moral ones? Propriety."

Con snorted. Motioned to himself. "Not in uniform, right? And I don't see any MPs around. Dude, I'm free. And you're killing my buzz."

Quinn's buzz was nonexistent, unless he counted the low-level buzz in his head that made him want to strangle Con and take him in hand in equal parts, and *fuck*, that wasn't good.

Instead, he went back to the truck, grabbed the itinerary that was Con's and handed it to him.

Con began to flip through it, standing under the lights of the Arby's in back of him. "Looks like our tour guide/ travel agent took care of everything."

"Yeah, these came this morning." Quinn had glanced through the itinerary briefly. "It's got both weeks planned, down to the hotels he's reserved and paid for."

Con sighed and stuffed the folder in his bag. "Are we set for tonight?"

"Hotel's an hour away."

"We're starting tonight?"

"According to Mr. Control Freak, yes." He glanced at Con's bike. "Want to stow this? I've got a cover for it."

"You ride?"

"S'why I bought this truck." He opened the flatbed and pulled the ramp down. Con wheeled the bike up easily, chained it in and covered it up.

Then he joined Quinn in the cab, sliding into the

passenger's side and dumping his camouflage duffel behind the seat. "She ride well?"

"Not bad. Better since I played with her."

"Gearheads," Con muttered, but he nodded with a smile when Quinn started the motor and it rumbled to life with a resounding roar.

Neither one of them was very talkative. They were both wound up from that last minute burst of adrenaline, and Quinn just wanted to get to the hotel before he lost that charge. With the radio pulsing some old school heavy metal—music Con didn't object to—Quinn tried to figure out the suddenly compliant soldier sitting next to him.

Scott'd never mentioned Con being gay or bi and it was obviously possible that he'd had no idea. Between DADT—because repealed or not it'd still been a part of Con's military life at one point—and the fact that these men were in one of the most gay-unfriendly professions, Quinn couldn't blame Con for not discussing his personal life.

Con didn't seem like he was the type to hide what he was, though. At least not off-base. While he could easily pass for straight, Quinn noted that, at least tonight, Con had made sure to catch as many men's eyes as he could.

Granted, Quinn had never come out and told Scott he was gay. He figured his family hadn't been able to handle the fact that he wasn't enlisting, and being gay would throw them over the edge. It wasn't a reveal he deemed necessary.

And the Dom part? Yeah, no fucking way.

Maybe he'd read Con's vibe wrong but, but…yeah, no. Especially not when Con had given him that smile and boldly looked him up and down.

Hell, had Scott known about him and told Con? Was this some kind of weird set-up?

Granted, if it was, Con had seemed as clueless about it as Quinn'd been. At some point, Con had started looking through the itinerary again. "Christ, he turned this into a military op."

"That he did."

"Well, this is what he wanted. Can't not comply with his wishes now," Con pointed out.

Two weeks. "Think we can make it in one?"

"And hit all the hotspots he highlighted?" Con shook his head. "What's the rush? I'm making the most of this—I plan to have fun in as many states as I can."

Jesus. Quinn rubbed his forehead. Nothing about this trip was fun, especially the endpoint. There was still time to say "fuck it," to get on a plane and show up, and hell, what was Scott going to do? Send him back to gather up Con? The guy was a grown fucking man in the Army, for Christsakes—he could get himself across the country.

And if he couldn't? Well, then maybe Con had bigger problems than Quinn should be expected to handle.

By the time Quinn pulled the truck into the hotel's lot, it was close to three in the morning. Con let him check them in, take the keys, sign for the room, and then Con followed him into the elevator.

The room was a two-bedroom suite. Con walked toward the room to the left immediately.

"We'll sleep in today and travel through late afternoon. We'll get to the next stop before nine tomorrow night and we'll be back on Scott's schedule," Quinn said firmly. Con grunted, went through the connecting doors ("Without shared suites you'll never keep track of him," were Scott's instructions) and left the door open.

Quinn glanced into Con's room and saw the man's clothes in a trail leading to the bed. And Con was only under the sheet—really, only partially under—and very obviously naked.

And there was no ink on his body at all—at least from what Quinn could see, which was three quarters of a solid body. That was a shame, because Con really had the perfect contours.

Stop thinking about his contours, Quinn.

But he couldn't stop. These next weeks would no doubt be a crash course in everything Con. And what an education it would be, if tonight was any indication.

And since his mind was racing, he did what he always did when he needed to calm the fuck down—he sketched.

He'd been born with art in his blood, and he'd been sketching from the time he could hold a pencil. He'd also liked giving orders. "Bossy as fuck," his father would say. "He'll make a good general."

He glanced back and forth between the bed and the paper in front of him, drawing freehand...and feeling oddly freer than he had in a long damned time.

ALSO BY SE JAKES

Men of Honor Series
BOUND BY HONOR
BOUND BY LAW
TIES THAT BIND
BOUND BY DANGER
BOUND FOR KEEPS
BOUND TO BREAK

Phoenix, Inc. Series
NO BOUNDARIES

Inked Series
HOLD THE LINE
THIRDS

EE LTD. Universe
FREE FALLING

Hell or High Water Series
CATCH A GHOST
LONG TIME GONE
DAYLIGHT AGAIN
NOT FADE AWAY
IF I EVER

Dirty Deeds Series
DIRTY DEEDS

Havoc MC Series
RUNNING WILD
RUNNING BLIND

Bluewater Bay (multi-author series)
NO EASY WAY (novella) in the *LIGHTS, CAMERA, ACTION* Anthology

WRITING AS
STEPHANIE TYLER

Shelter Series
SHELTER ME
PIECES OF ME (coming Fall 2016)

Mirror Series
MIRROR ME
RULE OF THIRDS
WALK IN MY SHADOW
DOUBLE BLIND (coming 2017)

Skulls Creek MC Series
VIPERS RUN
VIPERS RULE

Section 8 Series
SURRENDER
UNBREAKABLE

FRAGMENTED

Defiance Series
DEFIANCE
REDEMPTION
SALVATION
TEMPERANCE

Dire Wolves Series
DIRE WARNING (prequel novella)
DIRE NEEDS
DIRE WANTS
DIRE DESIRES

Shadow Force Series
LIE WITH ME
PROMISES IN THE DARK
IN THE AIR TONIGHT
NIGHT MOVES
LONELY IS THE NIGHT

Hold Series
HARD TO HOLD
TOO HOT TO HOLD
HOLD ON TIGHT
HOLDING ON (novella)

Hot Nights, Dark Desires Anthology
NIGHT VISION (novella)

Harlequin Blaze
COMING UNDONE
RISKING IT ALL
BEYOND HIS CONTROL

WRITING AS SYDNEY CROFT

ACRO Series
RIDING THE STORM
UNLEASHING THE STORM
SEDUCED BY THE STORM
TAMING THE FIRE
TEMPTING THE FIRE
TAKEN BY FIRE
THREE THE HARD WAy (novella)

Hot Nights, Dark Desires Anthology
SHADOW PLAY (novella)

ABOUT THE AUTHOR

SE JAKES is the pen name for *New York Times* bestselling author Stephanie Tyler, and half the co-writing team of Sydney Croft. First published in 2011, SE Jakes has quickly risen to be a bestselling author in the LGBT romance genre, as well as a fan favorite. Her books are frequently highlighted in *USA Today* and have been reviewed by *Library Journal* and *RT Books Magazine*. She's been nominated by several sites for Favorite M/M author and has finaled in the Goodreads M/M Romance Readers Choice Awards in 7 categories. She's a hybrid author who writes for Riptide Publishing and Samhain Publishing, and she indie publishes as well.

STEPHANIE TYLER is the *New York Times* bestselling author of romance novels spanning multiple genres, including Romantic Suspense, New Adult, Paranormal Romance and Contemporary Romance. She's a hybrid author who writes for multiple publishers, including Random House, NAL/Penguin, Harlequin, Carina Press, Mammoth Books, Belle Books and Samhain Publishing, as well as Riptide (as SE Jakes) and indie publishing. Her books have been translated into half a dozen languages, nominated for an RT Readers' Choice Award and garnered top picks from *RT Book Magazine* as well as starred reviews from *Publishers Weekly*. She's a frequent workshop presenter and has contributed stories for anthologies for charities, including **SEAL of My Dreams**, which has raised over 150K for the Veterans Medical Association.

SYDNEY CROFT is the alter ego of Stephanie Tyler and Larissa Ione, two *New York Times* bestselling authors who blend their very different writing interests into adventurous tales of erotic paranormal fiction. Together, they developed a world where people with extraordinary abilities, like the power to control storms, could live and work with others like them. The series has been described as "Erotica meets the X-Men," and is unique in its own "erotic superhero romance" niche. Larissa and Stephanie live in different states and communicate almost entirely through email, though they often get together for conferences and book signings.